"TIE THE MAJOR UP."

Locked in a small cell, Tyler Carradine realized the puffy swelling along his jawline meant some bones were broken. His feet were barely able to touch the floor, and his arms seemed to be coming out of their sockets from the terrible strain of supporting his battered body.

As he swallowed the blood still seeping from his damaged mouth, he heard the man keeping guard in the front room rise to the scraping of his chair. Tyler knew he should have expected this, the voice of Colonel Regis Wannabey telling the guard he could leave and chow down.

Unlocking the cell door, Wannabey tossed the ring of keys on an empty cot opposite to where Tyler was tied up. To Tyler's puzzlement, Wannabey had his hand wrapped around what looked to be a fancy Mexican spur.

"So, my dear Tyler, it comes down to just you and me."

A cold fear seemed to rip and tear at Carradine's heart. He could see that the rowel attached to the spur was what westerners called a jinglebob, that its points had recently been sharpened . . . and that his antagonist held it like a weapon.

"You haven't suffered enough." Wannabey brought the roweled spur across the chest of his victim.

THE JINGLEBOB MAN

ROBERT KAMMEN

ZEBRA BOOKS
KENSINGTON PUBLISHING CORP.

ZEBRA BOOKS are published by

Kensington Publishing Corp.
850 Third Avenue
New York, NY 10022

First Printing: December, 1995

Printed in the United States of America

Dedicated to Claudette Ortiz and the other helpful editors in my life

ONE

The man forking the spavined grulla ignored his hunger pangs and the itchy feeling caused by the worn collar of his patched shirt when at last the trail leveled off just after gouging through rimrock. Disinterestedly he reined up to let the hoss catch its wind after the long climb. Vacating the scrubby double-rig saddle somebody had dumped out back of Cheddar's Hardware Store, back in Gamboling, he flicked a finger to his forehead to brush the noonday sweat away while bending from the waist to check out the grulla's left foreleg. A few small blotches of blood clung to the bony growth that had formed around the hock. The hoss had started to limp bad, but if he took it easy, he might make it to the next town.

That'll be North Forty, he'd been told back at Gamboling— by his reckoning, still another fifty miles away. He was in no hurry to get to either North Forty or to any other western hellhole. Long since he had stopped trying to rationalize his feelings about anything. One thing, and only one, he knew with grim certainty: the hurt in him was still as deep, as canker raw, as it had been when he'd been festering in a Southern prison down in Missouri. Fate had dealt him the most savage blow it can deal a man, and it had left him with the embittered feeling that life was empty and meaningless, and that, for him, it would never be otherwise.

After a while, he got tired of staring at his backtrail, since the terrain thataway was dried out from lack of rain and the air around him was filled with gritting dust. Below the shaly butte, a series of red-and-black serrated ridges ran westerly like a rusted-out washboard. They were interspersed with scrub trees and mesquite and sagebrush, with the southern horizon hazed away as if a sandstorm was striking in, and with heat waves distorting his view. He was uncomfortably hot, mostly under the collar, 'cause that damned hostler had sold him a damaged horse.

At first he led the grulla at a walk along the disappearing traces of rutted trail passing over the ridge he was on. The valley ahead had more pleasant aspects to it in the ribbons of water coming off the mountains to the northwest, and down below, some draws were choked with scrub brush and grass and wild game, he expected. When he came to the north side of the ridge, he climbed into the saddle and brought the grulla down through boulders big as two-story houses. They were bigger'n any he had ever seen before and were just hanging there at odd, precarious angles, and he was glad when he reached the angling bottom of the slope and was well away from the ridge.

That afternoon and the next morning found him following a happenstance trail through timbered hills, and now, as he sat hunched forward in his saddle, he felt a lot easier, since he had come upon small bunches of grazing cattle and his hoss was still able to hobble along. He was hoping to run into some broke horses that had been turned out to pasture, his intentions being then to rope one of them and discard the grulla. Instead, the man's coal-black eyes pinched thin, studying the grubby layout hunkered on the rocky slope down there— -a shirttail outfit if ever he'd seen one. The soddies' chimney was a section of rusty pipe puffing smoke tiredly into the hot June air. Close by, a half-dozen horses, all flea baits, stood cropping idly at fringes of bunch grass along the line of a peeled-pole corral. Back of this a ways a small shed of a barn, its log rafters evidently poorly joined, sagged lonesomely on a slight slope sprinkled with scrub juniper and clumps of brier and blue-bunch wheatgrass.

The man on the grulla took time to pull makings from a pocket of his frayed long-sleeved cotton shirt and shape a handrolled. Now smoke strong with the scent of Mex tobacco wisped past his face as he gigged the horse and started it down toward the seedy buildings, a place reeking of poverty. What else could it be on this range, where sodbusters dug in at their peril, and even a decent-sized outfit was a gamble, bucking Carl J. Moore's long-established Box 7, holding sway on the eastern reaches of this large valley, and power-hungry Jax Faraday, the mayor of North Forty? Faraday had come in after gold had been discovered along Mineral Creek, and it wasn't long before his hired guns had blazed a trail of death among the prospectors. Just ruling the gold mining town of North Forty hadn't been enough, as now Faraday was buying up huge chunks of valley land and bringing in still more cattle. The small outfits and nesters either sold out at rock-bottom prices or were overrun by Jax Faraday's killers. This had roused Carl J. Moore's anger and opened his purse strings as he got into the game of buying land. Both forces were heading for one another, according to what he'd learned down at Gamboling. It didn't matter any to him if Faraday and rancher Moore killed one another. What *did* matter was that he might be able to find work at North Forty. At least for a while, at least until the urge to move on again became too overpowering.

With his horse scattering a few chickens picking at the barren ground, he brought it, limping, up to the door of the sodhouse, the grulla stopping of its own accord. He called out around the stub of cigarette dangling from his mouth.

"Hello the house?"

Immediately to his consternation the barrel of a rifle poked through the curtains of an open window next to the closed door. For reasons of self-preservation he lifted his arms, the sun hotter now and burning a hole in the nape of his neck. The curtains stirred, opened more, and he glimpsed the pale face of a woman with dirty dishwater hair. She yelled, "Who are you? I ain't got no spare vittles."

Carefully he removed the shapeless felt hat that had a leather strap below its crown. It had been the property of a recently demised cattle rustler. He had stolen into the undertaker's place of business after dark and taken the hat and a stout corduroy coat, which was now tied to the back of his saddle, even though punctuated with some bulletholes. "Name's Tyler Carradine, ma'am. My hoss has gone gimpy on me." He felt the heat of the cigarette starting to burn at his mouth and he spat it away. "I'd be willing to swap my hoss for one of yourn."

The woman stepped out of sight, then came fully out of the doorway, holding in rather capable hands one of those old but deadly .50-caliber Henry rifles cradled along the side of her aproned hip. She refrained from speaking but let her probing eyes take in the stranger.

What she was viewing was a tall, bearded man gone to waste. The eyes of the stranger had black pupils,

the whites shot through with red lines probably
caused by the harsh winds hereabouts, or by booze.
The full black beard was shaggy, and it came down
over the stranger's upper chest. It was streaked with
hairy white lines on either cheek and along the chin.
One white hairline pushed up to continue on as a
scar just nicking the outer corner of the man's right
eye. Without question, and she trembled inwardly at
the thought of this, the beard had been grown to
hide other scars. Probably to conceal just who this
stranger was, too. Back to his lackluster eyes went
her gaze; pity surged up in her . . . since she, too,
had felt the stinging lash of a man's hand to her
face. What settled it for her were the worn-out boots,
the left one torn open a little where it hooked onto
the sole. *A saddle tramp . . . that's all he is. And I sure
can stand some company.* She turned slightly, lowering
the barrel of the rifle as she said, "You can light
down, mister. Got some vittles warming on the stove.
Might want to wash up out at the pump."

Carradine led his horse over to the pump, where
there was a water tank. While the grulla drank, he
stripped the saddle away, laying the saddle and his
other belongings over where the ground wasn't soggy
wet and muddy. He came back and brought the horse
over and turned it loose in the corral, the other
horses shying away at first, then snorting through
suspicious nostrils as they came over to check out the
newcomer.

Carradine went back and got a bar of soap out of
a saddlebag, after which he stepped under the roofed-
over well. Drawing up a bucket of fresh water, he sated
his thirst before discarding his gunbelt and shirt and
turning to the pleasant chore of washing up. Except
for his hands, lower wrists, and weathered face, the
skin on his upper body was white but drawn taut across

his gaunt frame. His chest was matted thickly with black hair, his muscles were corded, and at the age of thirty-six, he felt old and washed out. He probably tarried longer than he should have under the soothing coolness of the well water, since he could feel the woman's eyes stabbing out at him from the cabin. Then, reluctantly, he put on his sweaty shirt again, as it was all he had in that department, picked up his hat, and hitched his gunbelt over a shoulder.

Coming in on the cabin, it was to find her appearing under the shaded porch, with him noticing she'd combed her hair and pinned on a yellow ribbon that trailed down over a slender shoulder. She wasn't pretty, but plain as all get-out, but now, when she threw him a smile, it seemed her whole face lit up. This told him that once she had been something special.

"Chow's ready, Mister Carradine. Might as well tell you now, my husband took off to try his hand at findin' gold up at North Forty. Oh, my, I'm Anna Drury . . . guess one has a tendency to forget one's manners after . . . well, chow's on . . ."

What he found upon entering the small combination kitchen and living room was a table set for two and a tangy smell coming from the pot of beef stew that caused hunger pangs to rumble up into his mouth. At her gesture, he took the chair facing the open front door. But before easing onto it, he set his gunbelt and hat down by the log wall. Along with the beef stew there was a pot of hot coffee and sourdough biscuits still steaming from being in the oven. In his wanderings the last dozen years, food hadn't been much of a priority. But suddenly he found himself eating ravenously, with juice from the stew trickling from his mouth. It was almost as if the smiles she kept casting at him released wellsprings of hunger, 'cause he was into his third helping before it struck at Tyler Carradine that he'd seen razorback hogs show better manners.

Lowering his fork, he mumbled, "Sorry, I . . . haven't had food like this in ages, I reckon."

She took mental note of his liquid Southern drawl as she said, "It does my heart good to see a hungry man set to like that."

"Reckon it was the food," he said awkwardly. He stood up from the sawbuck table. Staring at him now, she seemed to realize his height for the first time. A quick grin erased a little of the hardness from his wide mouth. "Obliged, as you sure can cook. Best I've eaten since— " His mouth closed abruptly. Then he reached into his trouser pocket, drew out some small change, and held this out toward her with a tentative hand. "For your trouble, ma'am." When she made no move to take the money, he placed the change on the table.

"That wasn't necessary. I suppose now you'll be heading for North Forty— "

"Figured on it. Won't get far, though, ridin' that grulla. All it needs is rest and a vet to treat its foreleg. Just how much further is it to North Forty?"

"About twenty miles; rougher country, though." She rose as he reached down for his hat and gunbelt. "Leave the grulla here and take one of my horses."

"Hardly a fair swap."

Again Anna Drury's unexpected smile seemed to light up the whole room. "You could throw in your saddle, Mister Carradine. I take it you're not from these parts— "

Busy with buckling on his gunbelt, Tyler Carradine didn't respond at first. Now, as he rotated the brim of his hat in his fingers, he stared down at her, wanting to find some excuse to hang around, at least for a day or two, just to savor her wonderful smile. But through the smile he saw the wary sadness in her eyes. "I heard about the trouble up here. Have you had any visitors lately?"

"You mean, someone wanting to buy us out? Shortly after my husband left to hunt for gold up at North Forty, a land buyer did come by. Didn't make much of an offer."

"Who was he working for, that Jax Faraday, or the Box 7?"

"He was working out of North Forty, I believe."

"Faraday, then." He looked past her at the cupboard and open pantry door and didn't see much in the way of staples. His search of the interior of the sparse sodhouse went opposite, and here he saw that some of her clothes had been placed into a large cloth traveling bag, which meant she was pulling out of here. And he couldn't blame her none, since spending any time at all in a seedy place like this could shorten someone's lifespan.

"None of my business, Mrs. Drury," he said, "but seems you're about out of food. Those hosses of yourn make tough eating. I spotted some big mule deer beyond yonder ridge. At least I can bring in some venison just in case you change your mind about pulling out of here."

"You saw that I was packing to leave. The truth is, my husband pulled out late last fall. More to the point, it seems he didn't want to drag me along. That he was tired of homesteading." She stepped out onto the porch, and within arm's reach of the Henry rifle, canted against the doorjamb, as if she still hadn't made up her mind about the stranger. The plain gray dress clung loosely to her lithe-limbed body, telling him she'd lost some weight. "Never owned anything before. To just give this place up . . ."

"Sometimes a person has no choice about that," he said darkly, letting himself go for a second back to sorrier times. "This place, not much good for growing oats or wheat; just grazing land. But you've got that creek yonder." He followed the slant of her eyes westerly, where the sun had pushed behind the mountains. "Well, I'd better pick out a hoss and see about one of those mule deer."

He came back about an hour after the sun had set to find Anna Drury sitting on a cane chair out on the porch. The rifle was there, too, and her knitting. She rose at his approach to have that smile break out when she saw the gutted-out carcass draped before him and more hunks of meat tied behind his saddle. He handed down some of the venison hunks and then swung out of the saddle. After he had brought all the meat into the sodhouse, he took the horse back to the corral and stripped the saddle away before turning it loose. As he worked the pump handle, the smell of frying venison came to him. This time it was his turn to smile.

They ate far more than they should have, washing the venison down with hot chicory coffee that he had dug out of his saddlebag, and they talked far into the night, probing at each other, finding out that they shared dark secrets, many of which Tyler Carradine was reluctant to disclose.

It seemed inevitable after this that she'd ask him to spend the night, and she did, but to Carradine's surprise, she also let him share her bed. Boldly, somewhat desperately, the words had come out of Anna Drury, to her greater surprise. She went into the bedroom first to put on her nightgown. Then he came in, hesitating under the glow of the coal oil lamp. It was here she saw the glint of sad despair in his eyes, and she left the bed to go up to him.

She cupped her hands to his face and said, "Tyler, we're recluses from an angry world. I tried holding my pain in . . . and had a miscarriage because of it." Now she led him over to the bed, upon which he sank, still clothed, and gazed up into Anna's eyes. When her encouraging smile appeared, floodgates opened.

"They were going to stand me before a firing squad. Men wearing butternut, same as me. My men, Anna, for somethin' I never done . . ."

Two

A former history professor at Southern Louisiana University, Major Tyler Carradine knew all about the Free State movement going on in Kansas, and this made him most apprehensive on this late-afternoon day in October of 1864. He had just brought his company into the bivouac area, which lay southwest of the Missouri and not all that far along a lesser stream, the Little Blue River.

In late August of this year three Confederate cavalry divisions commanded by General Sterling Price had left Camden, Arkansas. Accompanying them was Thomas C. Reynolds, Missouri's Confederate governor in exile, with the hope that this new offensive would reclaim Missouri for the Confederacy. Along the way, Major Carradine's company had been part of the forces attacking Fort Davidson, which lay twenty miles west of Fredericktown, Missouri, only to suffer 1,500 casualties, many of them regulars. From here they had followed the Iron Mountain railroad and destroyed the tracks to within thirty miles of Saint Louis. But to the chagrin of the Confederates, the city was garrisoned with a much larger force, pushing General Price to make a hasty decision in which he headed out across the heartland of Missouri, destroying as he went government depots and the supplies they contained, wrecking Pacific Rail-

road bridges and culverts, burning trains, and rob-
bing passengers.

Right now, Major Carradine was more concerned
with the immediate problem of seeing that his men
were fed and that a picket line was set out. Not all
that far away lay Jefferson City, the rumor floating
about that they would attack there, and by doing so,
face elements of the 2nd Kansas Volunteer Militia.
When he swung a leg over his McClellan saddle and
dismounted, it felt as if the saddle was still tucked
in under his stiffening legs. This day, by order of the
general, they had pushed it long and hard, a day
that had started out well before sunup. And Tyler
knew that if he felt this bone-weary, so did his men.

At least they had come in under oak trees still
thickly covered with golden leaves, and the ground
was carpeted with tawny grass. All around him came
the sounds of a large force picking out places to settle
in. He gazed back where they had just ridden to the
chinking sound of a rider spurring past: one of his
corporals. Deliberately they had held their horses
back from the river until the men could fill their
canteens and kettles, and as he began leading his
horse toward the riverbank, Sergeant Macon's voice
rang out softly, "Suh, I'll tend to your mount. Pretty
spot, now that the wind has died away."

"It is that." He smiled thinly at Macon, who had
prominent buck teeth and sandy hair and was about
the strongest man he had ever met. They were standing under an oak tree through which late-afternoon
sun filtered in ghostly webs of bright yellow light,
the bank of the river no more than five yards away
and already getting chewed up by the cavalrymen.
He had been through five major battles with Sergeant Macon, out of which there had sprung up a
bond of deep trust and mutual respect. He expected,

before this was all over, there would be many more battles. Or both of them could be killed in the next engagement.

"Boyd, what do you make of these Kansas volunteers?"

"Heard they're a raunchy bunch. All hot and heavy to abolish slavery and the like. Not regular army, though, Major, suh."

But, pondered Tyler Carradine, elements of the regular army could be mingled in with these Kansans, and as for the state itself, it lay just beyond the Big Blue River, which they expected to reach tomorrow. Troubling him always was the knowledge he would be fighting against men he had attended VMI with, those who'd kept their Federal army commissions. Old comrades, so many good times, before a medical condition known as arthritis had settled into his leg joints to end his military career. Then came the breaking away of the Southern states from the Union, with Tyler Carradine offered a commission, since men of his caliber were hard to find.

He went now to where the officers of his company had gathered by a campfire, just Tyler and three other men somewhat younger than he, but tried in battle. He declined the offer to share a flask of brandy and said, "It seems we're the western flank of the whole Confederacy, gentlemen. Sterling, you used to live, I believe, at Westport—"

"Yup, Tyler, place is situated smack-dab on the Kansas-Missouri border. Close to Brush Creek, which runs into the Big Blue River, about where Byram's Ford is located. But I expect you're more concerned about the men we might be confronting come tomorrow. Hardy folks, these Kansans. They'll fight. And die—same's some of us, I reckon, suh. It won't be easy."

"At least, I'm told, we'll be the superior force." He hunkered down alongside them, the heady scent of roasting pork coming their way. His men were good foragers when they weren't fighting. But pork, he knew, if he had any, would somehow really kick up the inflammation in his joints. The hand of Lieutenant Carlton came toward him holding a rather fat cigar.

"Spoils of war, suh. Please have it, as I liberated a whole boxful of these wonderful Cuban cigars . . . at gunpoint, I might add."

"Yes, I believe I will," murmured an appreciative Tyler Carradine, as from an angle off to his left he saw approaching them Sergeant Macon holding onto two tin cups. It could be that he was about to receive his daily dose of a concoction whipped up by the sergeant, of a tablespoon each of honey and apple cider vinegar blended in hot water. According to Macon, who had studied folk medicine a long time ago, this concoction actually killed the bacteria in an aching joint, thus temporarily relieving any pain. And it actually did work, Tyler knew.

"Squat," he said to Macon. "Or should I say, *Doctor* Macon . . ."

"Can't have my commanding officer goin' around grimacin' all day, can I, suh? Nossir, otherwise I might not be a sergeant no more. For I do truly love these stripes."

Somehow, at times like these, a great love for this way of life came over Tyler Carradine. Out on a campaign, there was a sense of urgency. You never stopped for long, just to make night camp, most often a cold camp, since smoke could be another enemy. This wasn't the case now, since every telegraph line stringing west through Missouri was telling of their coming. He expected sooner or later to be en-

gaged by troops pushing south out of Fort Leaven-
worth, that is, if these Yankee regulars could keep
up with the Reb's faster-moving cavalry. A bugle
throbbed upriver, its wavering notes hanging for a
while in the dusty air.

"Company, Major, suh."

Tyler Carradine looked past hunkered-down Sergeant Macon at three horsemen pushing toward them
through his company area, the presence of Light
Colonel Regis Wannabey signaling to him some un-
pleasantness was in the offing. The colonel was on
General Price's staff, and like Tyler, he hailed from
Georgia. In rising, he handed his cup to Sergeant
Macon, who discreetly faded away. His officers also
rose, and they would have left, except for a quiet
restraining word from their commanding officer.
Now he simply stood waiting, absently brushing dust
from the sleeve of his worn butternut tunic, which
hung more loosely over his thinning frame. He
thought, *Nothing will ever change between him and Regis
Wannabey. The man simply cannot forgive nor forget . . .
he nurtures his hatred like a ripening cherry. Clawed and
stole his way up to respectability. Has everything now, everything but MaryAnn.* She was waiting back in Atlanta
for Tyler's return, at which time they would be married. He loved her passionately, wrote to her when
he could, which in her opinion, wasn't enough. Yes,
once this bloody mess was over, she would be his.

Through the dust of the horses, he threw Colonel
Wannabey a cordial salute, failed to receive one in
return, let this go. The colonel sat regally erect on
a stately mount, a lean man possessed of bronze-
curled hair down to his shoulders. His tailored uniform didn't appear to have a speck of dust on it, an
illusion that pretty much, Tyler mused, summed up

the man. Wannabey had greenish eyes that never seemed to smile, especially now.

"Despite the fact, Major, we just went through a forced march of some length, you are to take out a patrol."

"By whose order?"

"General Price selected you personally, Carradine. You will not delegate the responsibility of this to one of your officers— you will command that patrol. Do I make myself clear?"

He knew that the general had issued no such order; the anger he felt was contained behind his bland and sunburned face. This wasn't the first time that something of this nature had happened. And to go running to General Price: no, dammit, no. "And this patrol is supposed to go where?"

"West, Carradine, to scout out the location of these Kansans. Push west until you reach the Big Blue. And we especially want information about Byram's Ford, for we might have to push across at full gallop. The sooner you leave, the sooner you'll return, and that better be before first light." Through the vicious glow that suddenly flared in his eyes, Colonel Regis Wannabey reined his mount around and away.

"Dammit, Major, that isn't fair. What a miserable . . . sonofa— "

"That we know, Sterling. Sometimes we have to remember that Wannabey is actually on our side." He hated leaving this comfortable campsite; all he wanted to do was to huddle in close around a fire and finish that letter to MaryAnn, if sleep didn't claim him first. "Select three men from each company. Have them report to me in a half hour. And make sure they've eaten and that their horses are fit to ride." As his officers took their leave, Tyler Car-

radine turned wearily and headed over to where his
tent had been pitched by Macon.

"I couldn't help overhearin', Major, suh. Sterling
was right, you know."

They shared a smile as Tyler took the tin plate and
fork and slumped down to rest his back against a
tent wall. He forked into the helping of meat and
beans, nodding when a cup of coffee was produced.
Then Macon said, "Lucky we've got spare mounts;
you want the bay?"

"Good night hoss, yes, Boyd." He rarely used the
sergeant's first name and had now, for some unex-
plainable reason. He chomped on the food while
watching Macon pick up his saddle and head to one
of the picket lines. Into his tired frame of mind came
a slight warning buzz of unease, which he let simmer
about for a while, trying to plumb what it meant.
"Quarter moon shouldn't give us any trouble. But
heading at night into unknown territory . . . consid-
ering that these Kansans will have their own patrols
out and about . . . just got to trust to God and luck— "

Embraced by the night and their own private fears,
the men, commanded by Major Tyler Carradine,
moved deeper into enemy territory. They had
ghosted past isolated farmsteads, guiding by the
North Star, and a quiet order or two from the major
about to say something to his ranking sergeant, when
the first traces of a road loomed up. Deep wagon
ruts stood out plain under starlight of a forlorn track
of road meandering up alongside a grove of trees
holding on an elevation common to the area.

At a shrill whistle from Major Carradine, the whole
patrol of twelve men slowed their cantering horses,
and at an arm signal, they began to cluster along the

fringe of the trees. They were quiet about it, as all of them were used to night patrols. "We managed to evade one patrol," said Tyler Carradine. "The Big Blue can't be all that far away. Can't miss the river, for that matter, as it lies due west of here."

"Wish there was more light, Major."

"Times you do, Corporal Benton. What troubles me is, we're just going in blind. Nobody has any idea as to troop strength or displacement." Before pulling out, Tyler had found out from Lieutenant Sterling that the Big Blue River ran deep and wide, and was, in fact, the last natural barrier before they stumbled over the border into Kansas. Though Sterling had volunteered to come along, in Tyler's opinion, the man and all his officers needed what rest they could get. "This could be one of the roads that cut into Byram's Ford. But to make sure, Benton, you take a couple of men and cut along this road, maybe a mile or two. But keep to either side of the road, as it has some twists in it, so you just might stumble upon an enemy patrol."

"Sure, Major Carradine. But you know, I smell trouble. I just know a lot of men are waiting out there by the Big Blue. Too bad I ain't a bird, I could sure use some wings t'night." In reining his horse away, the corporal leaned from the saddle and cautioned one of his men about some loose gear. Then the three cavalrymen were setting their horses into a chippy lope and were soon fading into the blackness of night.

After about an hour of steady riding, Corporal Benton could tell by the way his horse was acting that they were coming in on the river. It would be easier riding keeping to the road, but he'd obeyed the major's orders by slipping through the trees fringing on the narrow roadway getting a little wider. Back a piece there'd been a junction of two more roads hooking in, and even as dark as it was, he had picked up on fresh hoofprints and wagon tracks.

"A lot of traffic for this lonely stretch of nothing," he said to the private with him, and then both of them heard the incoming drumming of hoofs. He led the way across to join up with Private Kendall, the three of them fading in among the trees and shrub brush. Holding to their saddles, they unsheathed their rifles, but they wouldn't fire unless fired upon.

"Here they come."

"Just four of them, in ragtag uniforms."

"Got to be from that Kansas outfit," said Corporal Benton. "Ridin' kind of easy, like they ain't expectin' trouble. One of them's wearin' a big plumed hat— an officer for sure. Wait now, boys . . . wait until they come abreast of us. We need a live prisoner."

"Maybe we could capture them all?"

This decision was taken out of their hands when one of the riders on the road, who must have picked up on their fresh tracks, suddenly fired wildly in the direction of the three Rebs. This man went down first from a bullet lancing out of Corporal Benton's rifle. Then another man toppled out of his saddle, a third Kansan breaking back along his backtrail. But he didn't get far before he, too, was folding away and slamming into underbrush. The remaining Kansan, the officer, who'd drawn his revolver, was suddenly astride a horse that had gone loco, as it had the bit in his teeth and was breaking away at a mad gallop to the east along the twisting road, its rider barely clinging to the saddle.

Further to the east about fifty rods, the men, commanded by Major Tyler Carradine, tensed at the sound of the firefight to leave the road quickly but keep their horses surging westerly when the runaway horse appeared. Espying the Reb cavalrymen blocking its path, the horse muscled to a halt and reared up, throwing its rider out of the saddle. The man hit hard and simply lay there.

"Sergeant Robinson, go see what's happened up there. Then head back here pronto." Tyler spurred over and vaulted out of the saddle as one of his men managed to grab the reins of the Kansan's horse and bring it under control. Kneeling by the unconscious man, he lifted the dark blue hat away. He turned the man onto his back and was greeted by blood trickling down from a bad cut on the man's forehead. But the officer's pulse was steady, and he said to one of his men, "Not hurt all that bad. Different uniform than any I've seen before. We'll hold here until Sergeant Robinson gets back, and then return to camp."

"We're quite a ways out, Major Carradine. And our hosses could stand a rest, and they're sure thirsty, too, suh." He handed his canteen to the major, who splashed water on the Kansan's face. The blood washed away some as the man groaned and began stirring about.

"Our men are coming back, suh."

"Okay, load our prisoner aboard his horse. No sense going any further." Tyler Carradine walked his horse onto the road as coming in from the west he could make out Robinson's large frame astride the gray gelding.

"Benton and his men killed two Kansans; they brought this wounded one along. It was just the four of them, suh."

"This is no place to conduct an inquiry. Mount up, as we're cuttin' for home. Tonight, luck was on our side, Sergeant Robinson."

"Way it's been goin', we need some."

About an hour had passed, the men with Major Carradine aware that the Reb command would be on the move before they could get back to the Little Blue River, which would shorten the distance they would have to ride. The night before this one they'd gotten little sleep, and none tonight, and this was the reason Tyler'd brought them in the direction of a stream they'd encountered on the way out. They could build fires, since they were well away from the Big Blue and any enemy troops. The two prisoners, the enlisted man keeping up a continuous moaning over his side wound, rode back in the column. Once they'd been questioned, Tyler expected the prisoners would be turned loose— at least, these were the present orders issued by General Price, whose command consisted of more than 12,000 veteran cavalrymen, guerrillas, deserters, conscripts, misfits, and ragamuffins, separated into three divisions and accompanied by twenty pieces of artillery. It was officially known as the Army of the Trans-Mississippi. Though Price aroused blind loyalty and devotion in his men, he was cordially disliked by the Confederate president, Jefferson Davis, and virtually every Confederate general.

Some distance away, lightning erupted out of a dark cloudbank. It wasn't as humid on this fall night; still, the cold was coming on to wrap around Tyler Carradine, riding quietly out in front of his patrol. This helped to drive some of the sleep out of his eyes. He was continually squinting around, an old habit after so many skirmishes. Just ahead lay a long hogback elevation on which grew jack pines. He aimed for the rise and the stream passing along this side of it, his horse stumbling into a recession, but coming out quickly. Then he was in on the creek bank and everyone pulled up in a ragged line and saddles creaked when they dismounted.

Suddenly there was the sound of a body pitching to the ground from a saddle, a Reb spitting out, "That wounded prisoner . . . here, let me take a look. Be damned, Major Carradine, he's done expired."

Around Tyler his men set about watering their horses first and then tying the reins to convenient tree branches. In a little while, one campfire flickered into life, and another, the men digging out rations and cooking utensils. Though he was awful hungry, Tyler kept sitting with his back against a tree trunk while gazing at the dead prisoner, the other Kansan snugged up standing to a pine. *Probably never expected to die . . . at least as a prisoner of war. Heard a sky pilot say once the soul leaves the body and it becomes lighter, like it's just been relieved of a lot of sins.* He thought about Colonel Regis Wannabey. *Man whose body will be light as a feather when he dies. Wannabey just can't let go, leave the past be. Pulled some awful shady deals back in Atlanta. Bragged on this. Really was hot and heavy after MaryAnn— but she chose me. Got to ask for a transfer before long, or something is bound to happen betwixt Wannabey and me.*

"Here, Major, ain't much but it's filling."

He took the tin plate from Sergeant Robinson, who wedged in over by men of lesser rank. He was from a different company and held no allegiance for the major, nor did he intend to extend the hand of friendship, since officers often chopped away without caring too much. He would go his way, the major his, and damn all of it. Harney Robinson had been a roustabout on the Shreveport waterfront and a sometime pugilist, and at thirty, a lot smarter than when he'd joined up, three years ago. It didn't matter to him which side won the war, though he felt the Federals had too much overwhelming strength in both troops and equipment.

"Sergeant, I want to have a word with our prisoner."

"Shit," Robinson muttered under his breath, and for a while he kept shoveling the gruel into his mouth and sipping from a canteen cup laced with whiskey. He held there just long enough for the major to build up a head of steam, then abruptly left his eating gear and shoved to his feet.

Tyler had also risen, and he moved in on the campfire and handed his eating utensils to a private. Removing his weathered campaign hat, he ran a hand around the sweatband and was settling the hat back over his unkempt hair when the prisoner shuffled in ahead of Sergeant Robinson. Tyler said, "Private, see to it our prisoner gets some coffee." From here he turned to look at the Kansan, and just like that, Tyler Carradine's eyes widened in the shock of recognition.

"Gordy . . . I'll be damned. Gordon Laruby, it has to be you . . ."

"Yup, it's me, Ty, all right, sorrowful sight that I am." He stood there hatless and with dried blood still caking on his face, a blondish man with a long, horsy face and sky-blue eyes. Gray rode heavy along his temples and through his beard. He rubbed his right hand along his thigh, uncertain about what to do next.

And then Tyler Carradine took a giant stride to him and held out his hand, and their hands gripped together, silly grins breaking out in the awkwardness of it all. Once they'd been closer than brothers, serving together down in Texas and in other army posts before hostilities had broken out and men had had to make a choice. "You're with these Kansans?"

"Got severely wounded at Chancellorsville, I did. Crippled up a lot. So they cut me adrift. Came home to recuperate— home to Kansas, Ty. This uniform, rules don't mean all that much to the militia. And you, expected you to still be serving directly under General Lee— "

"I . . . guess things change for all of us. Oh, thanks, Private— here, Gordy, some coffee." Briefly his eyes flicked over to Sergeant Robinson, scowling darkly at what was going on, and angrily he ignored this intrusion, for all the sergeant saw was the enemy. A floodtide of memories struck out at Tyler Carradine, and sorrowfully he managed to push this aside.

"General Price commands."

"Somewhat lacking in experience, Gordy, I suppose."

"I hear he's not a barbarian."

He gazed down at the ropes wound tightly around Gordon Laruby's wrists, and he knew to remove them would provoke further glares not only from Sergeant Robinson, but from the rest of his patrol. At the moment, he was treading delicate waters. It was, he judged, sometime after eleven o'clock, and all of them were bone tired. "We might as well turn in. I'll take charge of our prisoner, as I want to question him further. Turning in means you, too, Sergeant Robinson."

"Yessuh, Major, suh," he retorted sarcastically. He was whiskey angry, which had served only to add fire to the suspicious nature of Sergeant Harney Robinson. But he obeyed the command due to his own weariness, and sought out his bedroll.

Tyler walked his prisoner over to the lower reaches of a short rise close to the campfire, the pair of them settling down stiffly. Adjusting his gunbelt to get his holster out of the way, Tyler lifted his hat away and dropped it down by his dusty boots. "This war, Gordy, isn't going to last forever. Did you know I resigned my commission . . . became a college professor?"

"Heard that, Ty, indeed I did. Tell me, when you lectured your students against drinking, did you recount to them some personal experiences of your own?" Gordon Laruby's amused laughter brightened up the night.

"I believe you saw the elephant more than I did."

"I did indeed, Major, suh. To become enemies— a damnable lie, Ty, a damnable lie. Not us, I'm hoping."

"You'll be interrogated tomorrow. By your enemy, other Rebs. Too bad that other Kansan died; have to bury him before we pull out. He'd probably have spilled the beans. But you, Gordy, no, you always were stubborn as . . . a Jayhawker." A thin smile trailed across Tyler's mouth. "But just what do we face?"

"What you face isn't just out here in the boonies, Major Carradine, but extends clear back to the Atlantic. This is just a fringe action, an unknown fracas in which good men will die on both sides. You Rebs have come a-conquering— we Yankees, a.k.a Kansans, just happen to have the stubborn notion that this isn't right." A few exploratory raindrops touched his face, which he brushed away. "Just a few lost clouds looking for a place to wet things up." He tipped his head to one side and gazed skyward.

And Tyler Carradine did the same thing, the rain increasing a little, mixed with the rolling of thunder. "You know, Gordy, I . . ." Without warning, pain stabbed at his eyes in the form of gritty sand splashing at his face. Briefly he was blinded, but he had enough presence of mind to grab for his holstered gun, trying to blink some sight back into his eyes.

"Gordy!" he shouted. "You haven't got a chance!" As his vision cleared more, he leveled his gun on Gordon Laruby, clawing through some pine trees toward the crest of the hill. He fired then, wide of his target. "The next one takes you down, dammit." He cursed as Laruby reached the summit and came out into the open for a moment, his back exposed, and an easy shot at this range. But Tyler let the moment pass, realizing to his dismay that he couldn't pull the trigger, and then Gordon Laruby had dropped out of sight.

"Uuhhhh!" Tyler Carradine screamed in agony, when the heavy stock of Sergeant Robinson's rifle slammed shockingly against the back of his head. He dropped heavily, not even aware of the hard ground coming up to break his nose. His blood spurted out errantly.

"Roust your asses!" the sergeant shouted out. "You, Corporal Benton, you saw it, how the major let our prisoner escape! Dammit, y'all, consorting with the enemy is a hangin' offense."

"Yo, damn right, I saw it all, Sarge!"

"Tie the major up. We're breakin' camp and headin' back." Stolidly he swung around and gazed down at the prone body of Tyler Carradine. Out of this he'd get some medals and maybe another stripe, his greater satisfaction that he had upended another Southern aristocrat. He hated the bastards with a burning intensity, and, gritting his teeth into a fanged smile, he brought his rifle butt squarely down at the unprotected face around the mouth area. "Eat tooth splinters, Major, suh."

* * *

In the old fieldstone jailhouse in the town of Carverville, the man locked in a small cell realized the puffy swelling along his jawline meant some bones were broken. He kept spitting out bits of shattered teeth. The worst of it was Tyler Carradine's being trussed up along a wall. His feet were barely able to touch the floor, and his arms seemed to be coming out of their sockets from the terrible strain of supporting his battered body.

The general had bought Sergeant Robinson's story in that Major Carradine had let their prisoner escape. And wouldn't you know, Colonel Regis Wannabey had wiggled his way into the thick of it, insisting that, since he had sent Carradine out with that patrol, the prisoner be placed under his charge. The only thing that had saved Tyler from the bullets of a firing squad was that General Price was more preoccupied with the upcoming battle.

Because of its location, Carverville had been chosen as army headquarters. Vaguely, Tyler knew that patrols in force had been sent out to discover that the Kansans had put up some fierce fortifications along the Big Blue River, even though they were outnumbered by the Rebs. They meant to fight, which greatly pleased the Confederates, since a good many of them liked nothing better than taking out more damned bluecoats.

Twisting his head to ease the pressure on his neck, Tyler went over in his mind the ugly details of last night. Colonel Wannabey had been in charge of an interrogation that had included two other officers. Tyler had readily admitted that the Kansan was an old friend, omitting to state that he could have killed Gordon Laruby with a shot in the back. What had, of course, sealed Tyler's doom— he would be facing a firing squad at sunup— was the damning statement of Sergeant Robinson. *For sure word of this will get back to Atlanta. MaryAnn, at least she still bears her name, will forget about me in time. Dammitall!*

He felt feverish; he hadn't been given any water since early morning. Through the one barred window came the sound of an army encampment, of men preparing to go into battle. Most of the townspeople had fled, and along the way, foraging parties had raided farm sites in search of food and had driven off livestock, which was plentiful in this part of Missouri. The men would eat good tonight, maybe the last solid meal for a lot of them.

It was getting darker in his cell, and these Missouri nights were getting colder day by day, especially for a man deprived of his tunic. As he swallowed the blood still seeping from his damaged mouth, he heard the man keeping guard in the front room rise to the scraping of his chair. Then, and Tyler knew he should have expected this, the voice of Colonel Regis Wannabey telling the guard he could leave and chow down. Probably come here, Tyler mused bitterly, to get in a last word. Then he took in Wannabey passing back into the cell block.

Unlocking the cell door, Colonel Wannabey tossed the ring of keys on an empty cot opposite to where Tyler was tied up. To Tyler's puzzlement, Wannabey had his hand wrapped around what looked to be a fancy Mex spur. "So, my dear Tyler, it comes down to just you and me."

"Water . . . you could at least let me have a drink . . ."

"I could. But for the moment I won't." He stepped to look out the window just as the sun was disappearing behind some tall oak trees planted in among the houses in the western section of this small farming town. He watched with quiet satisfaction the troops milling about company areas. His hands Wannabey had tucked together behind his back, a pose he often assumed. That he was enjoying the moment and what had befallen Tyler Carradine shone in his darkish-green eyes. He was not here to garner information from the prisoner but had come on his own to exact a revenge before the final act began in the morning.

"I don't understand them, Tyler. I am perhaps fifty times wealthier than you. Yet MaryAnn spurned me. Turned me out rather coldly when I came a-calling. I shall never forgive you for that." He wheeled away from the window after this harsh indictment, trying to control an inner rage, which if let go, would end this thing too, too soon.

"She didn't love you, dammit!" The pain of spouting out words brought sparks of pain swinging away from his jawline.

"All you had was the breeding, damn you. Where I had to claw my way to the top, to respectability. Not once did you or that bunch of snobs you ran with extend the hand of friendship. I swore then . . . well, as an old gambler friend of mine told me once, the odds always even up. But not for you, Carradine, not for you—"

For the first time, a cold fear seemed to rip and tear at Tyler Carradine's heart. How had a crazy bastard like this ever gotten a commission in the first place? Through his despairing anger he sagged down, unable to support his weight any longer. Shock waves tore at his shoulder blades, and he cut off the scream of pain. Momentarily he was blinded by this and the sweat stinging into his eyes.

"You haven't suffered enough."

The words didn't penetrate at first, and when he had blinked his eyes into wavering focus, there before him stood Regis Wannabey, holding up the spur he'd brought along. He could see more clearly now, see that the rowel attached to the spur was what western-ers call a jinglebob, that its points had recently been sharpened . . . and that his antagonist held it like a weapon.

The air in the tiny cell was rank with old scents, the only sound Ty Carradine's raspy breathing, the fear in him spreading like an uncontrollable fire. He barely seemed to have enough strength to pull back slightly from the hand of Wannabey, reaching in to rip his torn shirt away to expose more of Ty's heaving chest. Viciously now, Wannabey brought the roweled spur across the chest of his victim, the result a long, bloody wound that brought a muffled scream from Tyler Carradine.

"I love the smell of blood in the evening," Wanna-bey said through teeth parted in a pleased grin. He swung the spur again, at a different angle, across Car-radine's chest; the result were two X-shaped wounds. Somehow, this only served to whet his appetite to inflict more pain, more scarring wounds, only now his target was the face of his victim.

Before Ty Carradine realized what was going to happen, and blinded as he was by the crippling agony of being tied up, he seemed unable to avert his face from the oncoming jinglebob spur. The blow hit him first up near the left temple, then came raking down his face to cut away his facial skin like a knife going through soft butter. A guttural, insane kind of laugh-ter came from Wannabey, striking again at Ty's face with the spur, and again, through the sudden scream of agony.

All of a sudden, Tyler Carradine found through his disbelieving rage at what was being done to him the strength to rise up on the toes of his worn boots and release the pressure on his arms. As the spur started in toward his eyes this time, he yanked with all his might at the rope tied to his right wrist. The rope snapped, throwing Tyler around and in on Wannabey, Tyler's body half turning, his big right hand sinking into the other's thick unkempt hair. He managed to slam Wannabey's head face-first into the unyielding iron bars. He kept doing this even after the man went limp, and with Wannabey's blood spurting over his upper body. When he let go, Colonel Regis Wannabey slid dead to the floor of the cell.

Tyler Carradine didn't know that Wannabey was dead, nor did he care, for he was fighting away the shock of what had just been done to him; almost blind, sobbing through this he strained to free his left arm. When the rope finally snapped, he fell alongside Wannabey, totally drained of strength. He began hacking up blood, but still he lay there just wanting to die. After a while, Ty realized nobody was coming to investigate, and he must at least try to escape . . .

Rousing himself, he pushed to his knees and began removing Wannabey's outer garments and gunbelt. The process of putting on these items of clothing was painfully slow, since he now discovered that he had somehow dislocated his left shoulder. But when he staggered out of the cell, it was in the uniform of Colonel Regis Wannabey. At the front door, which stood open, he paused to lean against the door frame, realizing that air was coming out through a deep cut in his nose, and that he must surely look like a man who'd just been worked over by a butcher. But at least he hadn't been blinded, and now, as Ty Carradine glanced westerly along the front sidewalk, he could make out the saddled horse holding in by the jail wall. And he slipped that way and claimed the saddle.

He took to an alley and a back street that brought him ghosting through a grove of trees, hunched in the saddle and barely able to hold onto the reins. And then into a dark, cloudy night he rode, until he was well away from the town and those who wanted to put him before a firing squad, a man disfigured— of face, mind, spirit. In the days to come, he managed to avoid troops from both sides, and soon he was in Kansas, but clad in clothing stolen from an abandoned farm site. It was in Olathe and at gunpoint that he had the town's only doctor sew up his wounds. No anesthetic was used to numb the pain of the doctor's needle penetrating through the open lips of his wounds, and through it all Tyler Carradine didn't shed a tear or grimace, for he was a man who'd gone dead inside, carrying with him when he'd struck out across the western plains afterward just enough provisions to stay alive, guiding by the wintry sun. Another thing that Tyler carried with him, and which had been burned painfully into his mind's eye, was his glimpse of his damaged face in a mirror. It was right here that he began hating himself and all that lay behind him.

Now Tyler stared through the near-darkness into the attentive eyes of the woman, with him sort of lost in the haze of the past, and then he swung his head the other way. He picked up the threads of the story in the silence of his mind, just left himself drift to how it had been out in the Nations.

Three

A week or two later, Tyler Carradine was ghosting his gaunted cavalry horse westerly over the tawny plains. Far behind Tyler were the rugged hills and gullies of eastern Kansas, though he still rode gripped with pain from his healing wounds. He wore a gray woolen shirt and a shapeless felt hat he'd stolen from a farmhouse back a few miles, along with some food. There was only a little bread left and a couple of pieces of beef jerky. Hungrily he set his eyes on a moving object: a mule deer, he mused— but still out of range of his rifle. Sensing the horseman's presence, the deer bolted down into a bushy draw, leaving Carradine with a growling stomach and the ever-present pain coming from his puffy face.

As he rode, Ty Carradine could sometimes feel himself drifting over the edge into the dark pit of madness. Maybe he should just let himself go; maybe anything was better than his present state of mind. *I know troops'll be sent after me . . . as nobody kills a high-ranking officer and gets away with it. Even someone like Wannabey. Food . . . need that, an' some water for my hoss . . .*

Reaching up, he felt the puffiness that had partly closed his right eye. It was like a hive of bees were stinging away at his facial wounds. His jawbone ached, too, and every so often he'd spit that acrid taste out of his mouth. Neither this day nor yesterday had he encountered another horseman, the land just one rolling fold of prairie after another. The few trees he rode past were stunted, and the occasional draw had just a sprinkling of brush. Overhead, an afternoon sun rode across a section of sky unsullied by cloud, so that it seemed hotter to both horse and rider.

The horse kept on at a laboring walk, and then it was shouldering up a steeper elevation. Cresting it, Carradine was forced to rein up sharply, for he found himself at the edge of a dropoff below which lay the bend of a narrow river. His horse got to nickering and was eager to head on down. But not its rider, since he found himself staring with growing displeasure at a large body of horsemen taking their ease, the guns, some pointing at Ty Carradine, chilling him to the bone. He had the notion of wheeling away, but quickly discarded this when one of the men threw him a "ride-on-in" motion.

And he did, forcing his horse down the steep slope of about a hundred feet and onto the narrow floodplain. Ty held his hands up. Quickly his eyes played over the garb the men wore and their hard and distrustful faces. Some of them wore parts of uniforms, Yankee and Reb, and he realized they were more than just a gang of outlaws. He reined up while holding to the saddle, with most everyone there— he judged it to be at least fifty men— gawking at his scar-checkered face.

Finally came a jeering voice, "He's uglier than you, Bloody Bill."

"Ain't that the truth."

He motioned with his revolver for the intruder to dismount, and then he holstered his gun to come forward and yank the revolver out of Carradine's holster. "Over by that fire, ugly man."

As Ty Carradine was prodded closer to the riverbank shaded by willow trees, his horse bolted past him and plunged up to its belly to begin sucking in brackish river water. There were two other campfires, with the horses belonging to these men tethered along two picket lines. He studied the horses as something jogged at his memory, since the horses seemed to be in peak condition and had good bottoms and heavy chests. His fears were that this could be a band of guerrillas working under the Union flag.

The four men sitting around the campfire surveyed Carradine with cold eyes. One of them had used his knife to draw a map in the dusty ground. He was young, as were the others, and he was possessed of blond good looks rendered sinister by cold, heavy-lidded eyes. He said offhandedly, "What have we here?"

"I guess I blundered in where I wasn't wanted," said Ty Carradine.

"At least you're no damned bluebelly. Or are you?"

The blond man said, "He has the smell of a Reb." He studied Carradine's face, and after a while, he added, "It wasn't a knife that cut up your face like that. You came in from the east. On the run, I expect."

"I killed the man who did this to me. Unfortunately, he was a Reb colonel."

A slat-faced man wearing a low-crowned hat said sarcastically, "A damned deserter, Bill, will be no good to us. I say . . ."

"Easy, Cole Younger, simmer down." He chunked his knife into the ground and picked up his coffee cup, then rose and handed it to the intruder. He acknowledged the grateful nod with a smile. "I'd say you were also an officer."

"I reckon it doesn't make any difference now. You can call me Carradine."

"A fine Southern name." He gestured with his left hand. "What you see here is only part of my command. You are aware, I suppose, through your Southern newspapers, about how we guerrillas operate out here in Kansas and Missouri."

"I expect you'd be the famous William Quantrill?"

"Or infamous, as many out here believe. We use hit-and-run tactics; actually we've raised this to a fine art. Now, Carradine, what to do with you?"

"Meaning that either I join your outfit or occupy a shallow grave out here. I fled only to avoid a firing squad. I was a cavalry major, or still am, I suppose." He handed the empty cup back to Quantrill, letting his mind sort out all this. What troubled him was that Quantrill and his men had been taken into the Confederate regular army, with Quantrill getting the rank of captain. If he threw in with these men, chances were that he could be handed over to his old regiment. *Either death by a firing squad or a shallow grave out here. And Quantrill and his band of killers, they even murder innocent women and children. No choice but to throw in with Quantrill . . . and look to break away at the first opportunity . . .*

Instead of heading west, much to Tyler Carradine's growing worries, the band of Reb guerrillas struck to the southeast, mostly lying up during the heat of day to keep from running into any Union Army patrols. At dusk one night they ghosted into Cottonwood Falls, where their leader, Quantrill, took over the railroad depot just long enough to send out and receive a coded telegraph message, though they tarried long enough in this prairie town for his men to pull a few holdups along with raping some women. As they were heading out, the telegraph line was destroyed, and later on that evening, it was revealed that their destination was Baxter Springs, which lay at the junction of two other Southern states.

Forty-eight hours later, Tyler brought his tired horse along a dirt road paralleling the Verdigris River. Around him in the still of this humid night came the chink and rattle of other riders and the tattooing of shod hoofs. Moonlight was straining through rising fog caused by the growing chill, which told Tyler it had to be two, three in the morning, and a few more hard miles to go. Surprisingly, a whistle from the front of the column told everyone they'd be taking a breather, the riders wheeling as one, it seemed, toward the near riverbank and the beckoning oak and elm trees.

In Tyler as he loosened the cinch on his saddle was a sense of weakness and despair. Earlier in the evening he had managed to work out of his mouth a piece of broken tooth. Right now his mouth still ached, and he kept spitting out blood. Wearily he stepped to where his horse was drinking, hunkered down, and filled his hat with water, which he poured slowly over his head. This helped to cool him down some, and he did it again, the good feel of the water running inside his shirt.

"You, Carradine— lend me an ear."

Slowly he came erect and turned to look at William Quantrill puffing on a cigar, and Tyler was relieved that the man was alone. He went up to Quantrill, who led both of them under the spreading branches of an elm tree to a campfire that had been started. The pair of them squatted down, with Quantrill smiling at the coffeepot heating over burning pieces of dried wood. "Don't take my men long to build a

fire . . . guess practice is the trick. . . . anyway . . ."
He lapsed into silence while sucking on the cigar, a
dreamy, faraway glimmer in his set eyes. "Anyway,
early tomorrow mornin' we attack."

Again silence reigned, until Carradine asked, "Any
particular target, suh?"

"A target of opportunity. We need ammo an' rations . . . an' this army depot just this side a Baxter
Springs has that an' more." He shifted a little where
he sat to face Tyler more squarely. Now, somberly, his
eyes trailed over Tyler's marred face. "One look at
you, Carradine, an' everyone at that depot will sur-
render. I can tell, though, from your eyes that you're
reluctant to be a part of my command—"

"It's been a long war, Captain Quantrill." Hot cups
were passed to them, with Tyler gratefully taking a
long sip. "Found out I had to fight more than them
damned Yankees."

"Speaking of the bluebellies," smiled Quantrill,
"what do you make of that?"

Tyler followed the slant of the other's gaze to some
men just emerging from deeper shadows. He
counted at least seven men clad in blue uniforms,
with one of them alone pushing toward the campfire.
Closer, Tyler could make out Bloody Bill Anderson's
brooding face under the officer's hat. "All set, Bill,"
said the guerrilla, as he, too, was handed a hot tin
cup of coffee. Laughing, Anderson poked a finger
into a bullethole in the worn blue tunic.

"They'll never notice that," said Quantrill. And to
Tyler he said ominously, "The reason I haven't ordered your guns confiscated, Major Carradine, is that
come sunup, you'll use them against these bluebellies.
Make no mistake about that."

A chill running through him, Tyler could only nod
in tacit agreement. Then he was left alone when the

pair of guerrillas rose to stride away. Soon the order came to mount up, and the campfires were stomped out, and shortly thereafter, the guerrillas were strung out in the long line of travel, with scouts ahead along with outriders protecting their flank of march taking them southerly.

About an hour before sunrise a small settlement fell behind; someone remarked that it was Coffeyville. Soon they were on the main road marked with wagon ruts and deep ditches to either side and the pace of the horses picked up into an expectant canter. Out front about a quarter of a mile were the bogus Union cavalrymen. As for Tyler Carradine, he was gripped with some of the same excitement that shone on the faces of the men riding alongside.

Ahead, Tyler could make out through the growing light what appeared to be the black tops of buildings making up a larger town. Suddenly they were pulling back on their reins and fading off the road to the north a little toward a nearer cluster of buildings, and he figured this had to be that Union army depot.

Softly but firmly the voice of William Quantrill, who was easing slowly back through the column, told them to check their weapons. Tyler managed to dig his revolver out of its holster. He tried to imagine as he checked the loads in the cylinder that they were going up against regular army troops only to drop this notion, for a queasy feeling that something terrible was about to happen swept through his mind. Now, at the muted sound of a whippoorwill, they surged forward and through the open main gates, with Tyler staring briefly in passing at the sprawled body of the luckless sentry.

Without a word being spoken, the guerrillas brought their horses in and around two army barracks lying side by side. Shots resounded from another building, out of which an officer stumbled only to be gunned down. Lights came on in the barracks buildings, and a few soldiers managed to fire their rifles, but too late, as the superior force of Reb guerrillas had little difficulty in forcing a white flag to be raised. Through this, many of Quantrill's men kept pouring bullets through the windows and walls of the barracks, and then their guns fell silent when the survivors filed out of both buildings.

During the brief gunfight, Tyler had triggered off a couple of errant shots over the roof of the nearest barracks, and he held his gun low at his side now when the remaining Union soldiers were ordered by Bloody Bill Anderson to line up against the brick wall of a two-story building. By Tyler's count there were sixteen men, hatless and confused and about to die, when Tyler realized Bloody Bill was selecting a firing squad.

Terrified now, and bitterly angry, and with his blood running cold, he also noticed that all eyes were on the men standing by the brick wall, and he reined back cautiously. He walked his horse back around the end of a building and found the open main gates. Pain lanced into his eyes when the ragged volley of gunfire came, and savagely he brought his horse into a gallop back along the road leading westerly to Coffeyville.

Later on he would hear of how William Quantrill and his band of guerrillas had raided the town of Lawrenceville, Kansas. But at the moment, all of Tyler Carradine's anger was directed at just how horrible this war had become. *Brother killing brother . . . and for what?*

Four

Long before the sun had even the slightest notion of pushing over the eastern horizon, Tyler Carradine was on the move. Behind in the night inside her forlorn shack slept Anna Drury, unaware that she'd opened in Tyler a floodgate of bad memories. Tyler brought the hoss he'd switched to, a thinned-out chestnut, up to a steady lope across the valley floor, swinging it toward a low range of hills to the west, his face taut with displeasure at just how he'd let go with that Drury woman.

Simpered on like a wetnosed kid. Too late for me to go back and pick up the threads of what could have been. For a time he'd been a ranch bum. As quickly as he made a month's wages, he'd beelined for the nearest saloon, then hit the grubline trail again. Drinking helped him to forget, temporarily. But even temporary forgetfulness was better than none. His face gaunted, his eyes sinking bitterly deep into their sockets. Word about him got around, and spread owners began to give him a laconic "Full up" when he rode into their yards seeking work.

No longer able to get a riding job, and not caring all that much because of the risks involved, he hired on at odd jobs just for the price of a bed and a few drinks of rotgut. There were times when he could feel his body failing him, his limbs ached, and there was a winded feeling after a long ride. So he had no choice but to follow the seasons, leaving places to the south when the summer heat took hold, picking his way north as best he could. This was one of those times, but a little different this go-round, since North Forty was a spanking new mining town and there should be work even for him.

Switching his thoughts from his own miseries, Ty Carradine narrowed his red-veined eyes warily as he stared out across the valley solitude. It was about as peaceful as it could get. Yet it wasn't. For the arms of the Box 7 lay across this land like a greedy outreaching locust. He could sense a presence in the uneasy quiet, something he couldn't ignore as he spurred the chestnut away from the crest of a hill to keep from being skylined. Already, so he'd been told, the limbs of the locust were grasping, ripping away— an inevitable process of greed against these little chick-wire outfits that lay in its path. But where he was heading lay North Forty. And if the locust that was the Box 7 turned in that direction . . .

"The hell with it, it's not your worry," he snapped out into the darkness of the shadow, cloaking away from a hillock.

Sometime around late morning, Ty Carradine came upon a creek, where he swung down to fill his canteen. By his reckoning, he'd been saddlebound long enough to have traveled at least twenty miles. He should have filled his saddlebags with some of that venison, but instead he had pulled out quietly. He had never been long on goodbyes. Hell, he didn't even owe her that, this Anna Drury, especially not after he'd filled her pitiful-looking sodhouse with the ghosts of his past. And Ty knew, and damn to all of them, too, that they were still right here with him. What he needed when he got to North Forty was a long bout with some bottles of forty-rod. At least drunk he could shed some of these ghosts.

To his surprise, as Ty headed out again, the chestnut kept to a steady, untiring gait, and he figured once he got to town, the hoss would fetch him a good price. Before him the valley canted in a southwesterly direction between rugged hills capped with red and up there were puny fir trees. He liked the looks of this valley, one of several that covered the floor of this large basin. Snow lay heavy up near the peaks of the westward rising mountains, over which the sky was an azure blue. Soon the chestnut was laboring up a draw at least three miles wide, and when he'd ridden up a considerable piece, Ty reined up and twisted in the saddle for a backward sweep of the basin.

And right away, and to his dismay, he picked out the column of smoke smearing against the horizon to the southeast. *Her place; Anna's! Damned thievin' bastards have burned her out!*

Despite his anguish and his concern for the woman, Ty just held up there in the draw, indecision raking across his face. No doubt, he started to rationalize, she was dead by now. None of his business, and damn, he didn't owe the woman the time of day. Viciously he wheeled the chestnut around and up the trail he was following, knowing that in doing so he had sunk even lower. Maybe this was what Ty Carradine was really seeking, to find out just how low a man can get. Or how far a man can run. *Don't owe her or anybody else nothin'* . . .

It took a while for Anna Drury's sleep-drugged mind to react to what appeared to be the flickering light of a lantern reflecting against the yellow oilskin covering her bedroom window. As her eyes adjusted to the dark room, of its own volition her left hand reached out across the bed, groping for him. *He . . . he's gone?*

Puzzled by the outside light, Anna shoved the coverlet aside and pushed out of the bed. Crossing the threshold into the small living room, she hesitated, as to her there now came the tangy odor of smoke. Then she broke for the front door, shouting, "Carradine, damn him, he's set fire to the barn!"

Out a few rods and downwind from the burning barn, one of the three hardcases responsible for the fire and for rousting out the horses and turning them loose, sat on his bronc, watching the cabin. Another rider moved in closer. His name was Rafe Belsing, and he was also anticipating that before long, the woman they knew owned these sorry bunch of buildings would wake and bust out of the cabin. They were some of Jax Faraday's hired guns, come here to tell the Drury woman that her place had been sold out from under her.

"That barn was nothin' but an eyesore anyway."

"That it was, Carney. Was me, I'd burn that piece of crap cabin, too. But once cattle are brought in to graze, it'll be used as a line shack."

"What did Faraday pay her husband for this place?"

"Peanuts," chuckled Belsing, as just now he caught a glimpse of Anna Drury, in a white gown, staring in helpless rage at her burning barn.

"Here me out, woman!" shouted Carney Aker. "We work for the Box 7 . . . Carl Moore's outfit . . . come to tell you that this is Box 7 land now. Come to tell you to clear out of here." Laughing, he unleathered his six-gun and punched a couple of wild bullets after the woman bolting back into her cabin.

Unlike most people faced with a life-threatening situation, Anna Drury didn't panic. She slipped out of the gown and scrambled into a pair of worn trousers and an old work shirt. She was riddled with anger, some of it for Carradine, but a helluva lot more for her husband, who had told her before he'd left that he was going to sell the place out from under her. And now Ivan Drury had done just that, it appeared. To her, the bullets fired by that lowmouthed cowpoke were meant to kill.

With this in mind, Anna went into the living room and near the kitchen door lifted a shapeless felt hat away from a wall peg and hefted the rifle. Going on into the kitchen, she opened a cupboard drawer and took out a box of shells and dropped the box into a pocket of her patched denim jacket. From here Anna eased the back door open, and shortly she could make out a third horseman lurking under an elm tree, the sudden flare from his handrolled as he dragged in smoke revealing a stubbled face.

Anna crouched low as she slipped outside and was immediately in scrub brush growing around the back of the cabin. The man's horse nickered once, and he straightened a little in the saddle, checking things out. There was some light from the dying glow of the fire, and dawn was coming in strong, and so was Anna on the hardcase, the rifle trained on his chest from a distance of about ten yards.

"Don't make me use this!"

Startled by the woman's voice, he reacted by sawing back on the reins, his bronc rearing a little, the hardcase using this as a cover to drag out his sidearm. He damn sure wasn't about to let no woman get the better of him, as he'd be ridiculed unmercifully by his saddle mates. "Drop that rifle!" he shouted back at her, only to see a flame a split second later belching from the barrel of her rifle. He tried to speak, but it was damned hard when your larynx had just been ripped away and you were choking out your last gasps of life and blood. Lifeless, he pitched out of the saddle, and before the bronc could break away, Anna Drury had managed to grab one of the reins.

Lithely she swung into the saddle even as the other pair of hardcases, who by now realized something had gone wrong, had spurred their broncs into motion. In a moment Anna had found the other rein, had wheeled the bronc away, and was losing herself in the dense underbrush and screening trees.

When they found the body, it was Rafe Belsing who said laconically, "Strengthens my opinion that you never trust a woman."

"What now? Go after her?"

"Shit, Carney, we done our job. We head back to North Forty. That woman . . . she'll no doubt spread the word about this . . . about how these Box 7 waddies are on the prowl, killing and burning. Which is what Faraday wants everyone to believe. We'll have to cart the body off someplace and bury it."

"Why bother with that . . . ?"

"Box 7 headquarters isn't all that far from here. This fire, some of those cowpunchers could have spotted it; they'll be on their way over. And if they find the body—"

"Yup, I get your drift, Rafe. Afterward, though, we head back to town."

The draw, Ty Carradine discovered, followed a long series of rising hills stippled heavily with fir trees. The trail had widened into a much-used road replete with ruts filled with recent rainwater. Up here the air had freshened, and into his nostrils came the strong and welcome scent of pine. He savored this, and the rattling of a hammer against a nail told Ty he had reached his destination. Soon he could make out the sound of more hammers and the jack-hammering sound of a steam engine, which he soon found out was in operation at a small lumber mill. He rode on past, as coming toward him was a train of empty wagons pulled by big, rangy mules. One of the outriders threw the newcomer a hard look in passing, to have Ty Carradine seek the side of the wide road while avoiding the man's eyes. He wasn't seeking confrontation of any kind, nor for that matter, to strike up any friendships here.

When the wagon train was past him, Ty stared up at part of the mining town perched on a plateau extending out from higher hills. At the bottom of the plateau there were more log or clapboard houses and a narrow main street sloppy with mud. To the north the land pushed back up into timber growing thickly on escarping hills backdropped by the mountains. The place reminded him of Deadwood, in the Dakotas, and he expected the same untamed ilk was here, from backshooters to whiskey peddlers and rustlers, every man jack of them looking for an easy score.

Generally, he picked twilight as the best time to hit into a town, since people took to gawking some when encountering him face to face, and he tugged the brim of his hat lower over his forehead as he came upon, just past a blacksmith shop, a farrier shoeing a black horse. He rode into the empty lot and dismounted slowly while returning the farrier's nod.

"You want your hoss shoed, mister?"

"I want to unload this hoss if I can," Ty said carefully. He knew from the way the man was taking in his worn saddle rigging and clothes that the horse in question could be stolen. And stoically he pursed his lips as he started turning away, only to have the farrier cast him a friendly smile.

"Hard times an' me've been bed partners many a time, mister. I'm Virg Tugwater, a drifter, I reckon, same's you. That hoss is gaunted some . . ."

"Yup, I reckon some. All it needs is some oats and a curry brush and you'll find it's a stayer. Dead broke, otherways I'd hold onto it." Through a wondering frown he cocked his ears to the sound of bagpipes pulsing his way along the main drag of North Forty.

"That . . . one of Jax Faraday's boys heralding the arrival of the sainted one . . . Faraday himself. Along with being mayor, Faraday pretty much owns this mining town."

"So I was told," said Ty. "How big is this gold strike?"

"Reckon it's big enough. Folks are still pushing in here . . . and these gold panners are still finding gold nuggets." The farrier was about to say more, to tell the newcomer about how lawless this place really was, but he checked this away and instead added, "You oughta get at least a hundred silver dollars for your hoss, or more, mister."

Despite his customary wariness, he found himself drawn to the farrier, and he said, "I'm Ty Carradine, and I apologize for my crude manners."

"Look . . . Ty, one more shoe to go and I'm done. Upstreet a ways is where I've stabled my broken-down nag. Should be at least one empty stall left. Man owns the livery stable just might buy your hoss."

When they arrived at the livery stable, having passed along the eastern half of a long main street choked with saloons and gaming joints and thick with people, farrier Tugwater walked ahead of Ty holding onto the reins of the chestnut, bringing them around back of the stable and the open double doors. Here he told Ty that his present place of domicile was the upper hayloft. "Nary a room in town to be had, Mister Carradine. And if there were a vacancy, it would go at skyrocket prices. This damned mayor of ours sees to that. That empty stall'll do, I reckon, for tonight. An' I reckon you're damned hungry . . ."

Ty was certainly that, but the prices he'd just viewed affixed to some of the eating places they had passed were far beyond what he could afford at the moment. "Look, Virg, I've got some vittles in my saddlebags. Just you go and chow down."

"I earned two double eagles today . . . along with this I hate to chow down alone, Ty. I'm springin' for supper, at the Clementine Café, where works this biscuit shooter I've been sparkin'. Goldie, she calls herself. You know, I just might put a new pair of shoes on her before the night's over." The man's deep baritone laugh chased away some of Ty Carradine's reserve.

And Ty heard himself saying, though somewhat reluctantly, "Sure, Virg, I'll take you up on your offer." There was more than an offer of a meal here, in that he could worm out of Virg Tugwater a lot about the mining town of North Forty. Through the light of one lantern hanging from a support post, and that carried by the hostler moving away to get some sweet feed for his horse, Ty had been conscious of how farrier Tugwater had seemed to simply ignore the streaks of gray in his beard and the scar cutting down from his temple. The truth was, and Ty knew it, it was damned unsettling being in the presence of a truly unconcerned man such as Virg Tugwater. And dammit, he had no notions of how to handle this or thrust aside this iron wall of suspicion for the motives of any other living creature. He could have smiled back, but didn't. Instead, Ty pushed out of the stall and strode alongside the farrier out the back doors, not for the free meal, but for reasons of survival, towering over the farrier and others holding to the boardwalk they were now on.

"Tell me more about this Jax Faraday— "

"Vain son'bitch, for one thing. Got this town in an iron grip, what with all these hardcases he's brought in. The miners know this, that the games are rigged; still they keep comin' back for more. Downstreet, that big pine-sided building, the Carousel Emporium— Faraday's headquarters."

"A funny name for a Scotsman."

"Doubt if he's that, Carradine. Maybe he just likes bagpipe music, along with cheatin' these miners. Two years ago North Forty wasn't much, Isaac Turner's roadhouse, couple of stores, about all— now look at it."

"Too many buildings tucked in here, I figure."

"A real firetrap," Virg Tugwater agreed. "And the gold; some of the miners tell me there isn't all that much, but still those newspaper advertisements put out by Faraday keep drawin' them in."

FIVE

Over in his office at the Carousel gaming emporium there was another man who shared the farrier's opinion that less and less gold was being found along Mineral Creek. Only for Jax Faraday there was no sense of worry, for in the eighteen months that he'd settled in here, he had amassed a considerable fortune. He figured he could milk time out of this— a year, maybe less— if the miners gave up and headed out to another mining area.

Faraday had plowed a lot of this money into acreage in the basin, which included his buying several small spreads and homesteads. This acreage was, for the most part, located along waterways, for without water the land was practically useless. Though he also owned wholly or in part most of the businesses in North Forty, it was the *Mineral Tribune,* as yet the only newspaper in the basin, that he considered to be at the heart of his power. Barely a year old, the newspaper had been started by a man no longer residing, for reasons of health, out here in the basin. The man had been cowed into selling the *Tribune* to Faraday for one-tenth its value. Through its pages Jax Faraday kept his new editor pounding away with articles denouncing the crooked methods used by the Box 7 to buy land. There had been one encounter between Faraday and rancher Carl J. Moore, a bloodless affair of shouted accusations. Ever since, Moore had kept clear of North Forty, and this worried Faraday, since he knew Carl Moore to be an unforgiving individual. It was after this confrontation that both men got busy buying up land, each of them determined to be the biggest cattleman in the basin, spurred on by the news that the Union Pacific had decided to run their main line through southern Wyoming.

Jax was a big man, and handsome in his way, with his wavy blond hair, though the green eyes were coldly centered in his heavy-jawed face. But at only forty-one, he had a face that had already begun to show a faint jowling. Where once, muscle had packed his heavy frame, now it was fat, and he wasn't all pleased with this, nor with having to get his tailored suits cut a little bigger. He had it in mind to get out more to check on his ranching operation instead of wasting his time at the card tables. He was realizing that a lifetime of bad habits was hard to break.

To make the room larger, the connecting wall of another room had been removed. Now Faraday could step directly into his bedroom suite. The main windows lay to the south, with the curtains pulled aside, as he liked to have sunlight pour in. Most of his years had been spent down in southern Texas and New Mexico, and even though it was a warm day, flames were eating away at a log in the fireplace. The hardwood floor was bare and boot scuffed. A big, black Grimes Brothers safe hogged the northwest corner of the office. There was the one desk and some hardbacked chairs, and of course, an oaken drop-leaf table fixed up to hold his ample supply of expensive liquors.

The woman by the table was mixing a drink for Faraday while half listening to the open conversation between Faraday and a hulking man named Harney Robinson. Like Jax, he spoke in a Southern drawl, which at the moment held a mingling of contempt and unanswered questions as he added to what he'd said before. "Last I seen of Ivan Drury, he was hanging around them cheap Northside dives, spoutin' out some mighty dangerous words . . ."

"Relax, Harney, nobody ever listens to the mindless ramblings of a drunken sodbuster. Once Drury unloads the money I paid him for his place, he'll drift out of here. He's probably bitchin' 'cause he sold out too cheap. If we kill him, the stink about it'll probably get to Cheyenne, fetch out a damned U.S. marshal. Been too many killings lately."

"But most of them outside of town, by road agents supposedly unknown to you, Jax." He was second-in-command to Faraday, and much bigger, and with a face marked by years of lacing down cheap corn liquor. His eyes lay buried between deep folds of flesh burned by the wind and sun, and Harney Robinson wore rough clothing, and a gun thonged down at his right hip. Instead of heading back to Alabama during the last days of the Civil War, he'd simply deserted and headed west until encountering the Rockies. And Jax Faraday was dealing cards in a Pueblo gaming hall. Tales of a rich gold strike at North Forty had brought them here.

"Okay, we leave that sodbuster alone," Robinson said, even though he had no intention of doing so. Like Faraday, he was investing a good share of his money in land that lay up near the southern reaches of the Wind Rivers, by a large lake. A lot of that acreage wasn't of much value, and even a mountain goat would have a hard time existing up there, but Harney Robinson figured that someday he could turn a profit if anybody wanted to fish at his lake. Fishing to him was a way of life, but meanwhile, a man had to hack out a living.

"That strong enough, sugah?"

"Just right, Thelma." Faraday smiled. "Belsing and the others should be pulling in before long. Watch for him when you're down there . . . an' keep an eye on that new dealer, what the hell's his name . . ."

"Lindahl, or so he said," she threw back across the threshold.

Sipping from his glass as he rose, Jax Faraday strode over to gaze out a window at the congestion on Main Street. Though he felt satisfied at what he saw, burring at his mind were thoughts of the Box 7 and rancher C. J. Moore. Moore was nobody's fool, and the man was also a considerable political power in these parts.

"Well, I'll be leaving."

He turned and said to Robinson, "That sodbuster, Drury, if you do run across him, head him out of town. Alive, you hear?"

The main diggings along Mineral Creek started about a quarter of a mile northwest of town and were strung from there for at least a half-dozen miles along a stream dried up considerably since spring runoff. Other, lesser claims could be found on two smaller creeks cutting away to either side. Now, as the sun sank away and ended another bleak day, a considerable number of miners either began hoofing it on foot or rode in to get a hot meal or to gamble and drink.

One of them, a man who'd been a bricklayer back in Hershey, Pennsylvania, checked out the loads in his Winchester as he passed with others along a worn trail running adjacent to the creek. It was at night that road agents liked to prey on small groups like this, and the seven men bunched together, and afoot, were grimly determined they'd spill out hot lead at the first sign of trouble.

Former bricklayer Henry Atwood had left his partner back guarding their claim, and he wouldn't be going in, except that working a sluice not only wore out a man, but made him chow down heavily. The fact was, they were down to their last five-pound sack of flour and had plumb run out of salt. He didn't particularly cotton to paying through the nose for these and other items in North Forty. Either that or starve, as game, deer, and antelope shied away from these parts after being hunted so much. Beefsteaks were up to fifty bucks a pound.

"Sons of bitches," he cursed.

"What's that, Atwood?"

"Heading into North Forty, where every merchant is kin to these road agents, goes agin the grain. But either that, or eat grasshoppers. Stupid as all get-out, that's what mining is all about. Boils down to these dipshits letting us humble miners dig out the gold."

"Then in order to survive, we simply fork it over for vittles and such."

"This Jax Faraday . . ."

"Mayor, my cold, achin' butt— he's involved in some damned crooked dealings. Got to be."

"Got hisself an army of gunslingers. Be courting suicide going against them. About the only answer is that a man pulls out of here."

Atwood knew the other seeker of gold nuggets was right as rain, a thought that stuck with him as he came over a low rise and was all of a sudden on the outskirts of North Forty. Lights and sound from the boomtown reached out like bloodsuckers to cause a lighter and faster footfall, and eagerly they forged onto Main Street. And as Atwood picked up his gait to keep up, he had to veer slightly to avoid running into a tall bearded man. Just for a moment he took in the streaks of gray in the beard of Tyler Car-

radine, then the two men were passing one another
in wary silence.

Back at that café, Tyler hadn't felt all that comfortable under the wondering eyes of other diners and
that waitress the farrier liked. So as apple pie was
about to be served, he made some lame excuse to
Virg Tugwater and vacated the café, going from there
to a saloon. The whiskey bottle he'd purchased lay
heavy in one of his coat pockets, his intentions being
to head back to the livery stable and lose himself in
a whiskey haze.

*Anna Drury . . . too bad about her. But she knew the
risks out here. An' this North Forty, somethin' about it I
don't like . . . should pull out once I sell that hoss . . .*

As Tyler Carradine passed along the fringe of
boardwalk opposite the Carousel Emporium, the man
who'd just emerged from the building stepped to the
edge of the overhanging porch and surveyed the
street, lighting a cigar. Briefly, his eyes brushed over
Carradine ducking onto a side street, and then
Harney Robinson muttered derisively, "Now, there
goes a real saddle bum." Any remembrance of former Reb officer Tyler Carradine had faded from his
mind, as had thoughts of the war. Out here, nobody
knew or cared that he had been a Reb sergeant, or
whether you lived or died. He liked it this way.

As he was on the verge of checking out the Northside saloons in hopes of running into this mouthy
sodbuster Ivan Drury, the sight of two horsemen loping in from the east brought from Robinson a wondering grunt, as three had gone out and only two
were coming back. When Rafe Belsing spotted Robinson, Belsing angled further along the block and
reined up to stare back. "We lost a man."

"Yeah?"

"Don't worry, Harney, he's buried where nobody'll find him."

"An' the sodbuster's wife— "

"Got a mighty fine set of lungs on her," grinned Rafe Belsing. "She'll make damn sure everybody knows it was the Box 7 that burned her out."

"Good, now I've got another chore for you men."

"Dammit," muttered Carney Aker, "we need some chow, an' our hosses are worn out."

"Aker, you always were a lazy bastard," snapped Robinson. "Tend to your hosses and after you've et, I want you to help me find Ivan Drury."

"Yeah, I remember him . . . runty, with a shaggy reddish beard and a shitty smile. So then, if we run into him?"

"Hold him for me," Harney Robinson said darkly, as he pushed out into the street. He saw no reason to detail his reasons to men of lesser intelligence such as Belsing and Aker. Men like them rode and lived hard and died young. *Shortchangin' themselves right into the grave.*

Six

Oldtimer Stony Abernathy had worked for the Box 7 longer than the other hands, over twenty years, as a matter of fact, so Stony knew pretty much the mind twists of rancher Carl Moore. He knew that Moore wasn't going to sit around much longer and just let Jax Faraday keep on putting out poisonous editorials depicting the rancher as being lower than a sidewinder. In his younger years, Stony knew, C. J. Moore would have hammered the bejesus out of Faraday and probably burned down that newspaper building over in North Forty.

He was riding a little behind Moore at the moment, as it was Stony and Moore and a cowpoke handling the reins of a team pulling a wagon, the three of them on their way over to Rattler Creek. Abernathy was a dried-out man in his late forties, with a face pitted and burned and generally creased in a smile. It was Moore who'd took him in, even though Stony had just been released from state prison, as he saw something in the young man others missed. And it was Carl Moore telling Stony that he'd better shed that bitter scowl and get to smiling. Stony began doing this to soon discover that a grin sure made a lot of people stop and ponder just what the hell that grin was all about, that maybe Abernathy knew something others didn't.

What he knew, and this was acquired over the years, was that Carl Moore had a heart of gold, though he had gruff mannerisms and didn't particularly cotton to saddle tramps dropping in that much, though he never turned one away. A blocky man in his early fifties, Moore was concerned for his ailing wife, Olga, a spirited woman everybody in the basin liked. But the shank of his worries right now were for that nester family still holding in by Rattler Creek. Under the low-crowned cattleman's hat his china-blue eyes pierced beyond his worries of the moment to take in some of his cattle pushing into a distant arroyo.

He was the biggest rancher in the Bridger Basin of southwestern Wyoming only because his only brother, Orv, had died after being gored by a bull suddenly gone loco. Orv's holding had consisted of nearly two hundred thousand acres, his will leaving everything to Carl, a windfall that put his total acreage at about a half million. It had taken him a long time to get over Orv not being around to argue with, or just to head into one of the small cowtowns in the basin and go on a bender with. Then life had been mighty good.

"Now I have Faraday to cope with," Carl Moore said softly, as Stony pushed in alongside. A week ago he had bought out another homesteader, Sven something-or-other, and out of Minnesota. *Man's a black dirt farmer. But he had to drag out his five yonkers and take a stab at gettin' some free land. Can't blame him none. Pity his wife had to up and pass away this spring. Broken heart, maybe, life too hard for her, maybe pining away for those Minnesota lakes and forests.* Moore had paid more than the market price for the Swede's small parcel of land, and he was on his way now with his wagon to make sure the family at least had a ride down to La Barge, as the homesteader only had the one hoss, one he'd used to pull his plow and do other chores.

"Whatcha make of that, Carl?"

"What have you got, Stony?"

"Rider just pushed out of that draw; still too far away to make him out. Didn't think we had any Box 7 hands up thataway."

"We don't." Carl Moore looked back with some concern at the waddy reining his team of horses through a high rise covered with shaly rocks. He felt easier when they'd worked down the slope and were loping across open prairieland under scattered clouds, and with Moore setting his eyes back where they'd seen that horseman.

He finally said, "Probably a saddle tramp."

"Or somebody on their way to North Forty."

"To Helltown," he muttered. He didn't smoke, but chewed tobacco, his displeasure causing Moore to dip a hand into a shirt pocket and lift out a large plug, which he bit into. "Faraday thinks by clouding my name, Stony, everybody's gonna sell out to him. Painted me dark, he has. Back East you'd sue a man for slander."

"I know you, Carl"— Stony Abernathy's smile widened— "you've got somethin' devious in mind for Faraday . . ."

"A lot of men are being killed over at North Forty— miners, mostly. Generally happens in a boomtown. Word is, Stony, Faraday controls just about everything up there. I did get word to the U.S. marshal's office. They'll send in somebody. But I figure sooner or later, Faraday'll make that fatal mistake. And it won't be me killing him, but one of his own."

"You reckon that's what'll . . ." The rest of it was

choked off by Stony Abernathy as a horseman suddenly loomed out of a hidden draw and was in on them, the horse pulling up quickly in the confusion, so fast that the person riding it was pitched out of the saddle and almost into the protesting hoofs of the horse ridden by Stony. "I'll be damned . . . a woman?"

Stunned by her sudden encounter with the sandy ground, the wind knocked out of her, Anna Drury tried rising, only to flop down again, and with fear over the unexpected encounter throbbing at her temples. Her one thought was that if it was the same men who'd burned her out, she was about to be molested and killed. Then the sonorous voice of Carl Moore penetrated her thinking.

"Ma'am, we're awfully sorry . . . there, Stony, go after her horse . . ." He'd swung down and left his ground-hitched bronc to move in and bend from the waist as the woman spun like a cat onto her back and stared up at him. "Ma'am, I . . . I'm Carl Moore . . . from the Box 7. We . . ."

"You sonofabitch!" Anna Drury found herself scrambling up from the ground and flailing her clenched fists at the man she believed had burned her out. A blinding anger distorted her face, and if she'd been packing a gun she'd have killed this monster. "You burned down my barn! You took my horses! Damn you, anyway!"

Somehow Carl Moore managed to evade her windmilling arms and wrap his own arms around her upper body, saying, "Lady, simmer down, dammit. Just what the hell is this all about?" He was angry now, and fighting mad.

Slowly Anna let it sink in that the man holding her wasn't going to do her any harm. And through a deep outpouring of angry air, she stopped struggling as she tried to compose herself and her thoughts. In fact, this man was old enough to be her father. It was now that Moore released his grip and stepped back cautiously a pace. Turning, she regarded him in icy silence.

"So, what in tarnation is this all about?"

"These men said they were from the Box 7. That my husband had sold our property."

"Which is a homestead, I reckon?"

"Was— now you own it."

"Nope, not me, ma'am. Just whom am I talking to?"

"A pissed-off Anna Drury."

"I surely can see that. Can you describe these men?"

"Not worth a damn, Mister Moore. They rode in before sunup."

"Drury? Seems to me you folks set up shop southeast of here, as I recollect. I have to tell you, Mrs. Drury, this gent named Faraday, out of North Forty, is buying up land." His eyes flicked to Stony holding onto the reins of the woman's horse and drawing up a short distance away. "Anyway, it saddens me to see a woman so blamed upset, and way out here by her lonesome."

"You're saying, Mister Moore, you didn't buy our property from my husband— "

"I reckon I didn't, ma'am," he said soberly. "Believe this, too— I believe in the Christian way of doin' things. Your husband, it appears he done run off and left you to handle things . . ."

"He did," Anna admitted, around a forced smile of resignation. "Went to North Forty."

"The devil's playground." He smiled back at Anna, marveling at how her smile seemed to make everything right. This was a woman with grit, and he knew a moment of crisis had passed. However, his very nature made Carl Moore realize he couldn't let it or her go just like that. "I expect, ma'am, you're headed for North Forty?"

"I am."

"Alone, and about busted, I expect."

"Stone broke, but I'll manage." She leaned to pick up her hat, and when she straightened up, it was to stare in puzzlement at the sight of the rancher pulling out his leather billfold.

"I . . . please, I'll . . ." she began.

"No, Anna, you won't. What I got pieced out is that your husband sold your place out from under you. And if you *do* find him, he'll be busted." The two hundred in greenbacks he removed was placed quickly into her hand, with Carl adding softly, "Even this won't last all that long where you're goin', Mrs. Drury. And it's no loan either . . . just that you're too much of a lady to . . ."

Through the tears erupting from her eyes, Anna Drury threw her arms around him, clinging tightly to this island of support in this hostile land. Somehow she managed to regain her composure, and when she did, she pulled away and gazed up at his pensive face. "I will pay you back, Mister Moore, every red cent of it."

He just nodded at this as Anna Drury reclaimed the saddle and took the reins from Stony Abernathy astride his bronc. As they rode, Carl Moore pointed out some landmarks that would help her find the road that curled into North Forty. In his calming presence, Anna spoke about how tough it had been for her as a homesteader, and then she said, "Night before I was burned out, I let this saddle bum stay overnight. Maybe you know him— Tyler Carradine?"

"Reckon I don't, Anna. A lot of men are drifting

through, headin' for North Forty. Well, it's goin' on mid-afternoon, and yonderly is that draw that'll take you to the main road. You know, I could send Stony here along to see no harm comes to you . . ."

"That won't be necessary. I'm a damned good rider." Now concern flickered in her eyes. "That man I shot at back there, he went down hard. I . . . I wish it had been otherwise . . ."

"That jasper knew the risks of what he was doing, so don't fret about him. Anna, got this feelin' we'll bump into one another again."

"Yup," agreed Stony, "so long, ma'am."

Anna Drury left behind one of her sparkling smiles as the horse responded to the jab of her bootheel. The men held their horses to a walk until Anna had passed through the draw and was dropping further into a low valley, and then Carl Moore murmured, "Homesteaders . . . wish they were all as pretty as her. They sure bring trouble, though, Stony."

SEVEN

He kept threshing about on the protesting springs of the narrow cot, thinking he was drowning, trying desperately to come out of the black pit of drunkenness. Finally, frantically, Tyler Carradine managed to sit bolt upright on the cot and to push away the panic shining out of his bloodshot eyes. When he did, the wetness was still there in the form of rainwater seeping through cracks in the roof.

"Damn . . . where am I?"

He found he had trouble remembering his name, much less that he'd squandered the money the hostler had paid him for his horse. His head felt bigger'n a washtub, and he stank all over, as did this squalid room in some hellish roominghouse or hotel. Even his teeth ached, so he knew this had been one hell of a bender. He tried standing, only to weave away from the cot and slam into an old unpainted dresser, and as he did, someone began hammering at the door.

"What the hell?"

"You, cowboy, time to vacate your room!"

"It ain't locked."

The door swung open and Tyler gazed sullenly at the middle-aged man holding a Greener with a practiced casualness, while behind him lurked an older man with a startling thatch of snowy white hair. "Five in the morning, drifter."

"So?"

"You're stone broke, so just ease out of my hotel." The foxy grin held as Tyler Carradine swung toward a broken chair, picked up his coat, and started pawing through the pockets in search of some loose change.

"You were broke two days ago. Sold me your gun then, for a couple more days to sack in here and for some booze. Come on now, saddle bum, don't make me paint your blood all over that wall."

"All right," mumbled Tyler, as he shoved the chair aside and found his shapeless hat. "All right . . . you cheap tinhorn . . ."

Out in front of the hotel, which he learned from the sign was called the Commodore, the rain really came in on him, pelting down big, sleety drops that stung when they hit flesh. And it was colder than he liked it. He stumbled in closer to the wall because the overhanging porch was as leaky as the room he'd just vacated, trying to get his bearings. Trying to think through the lingering effect of the whiskey still numbing his brain. About all that registered was that he wasn't hungry, and that if he was near a high cliff, he'd jump and get this over with.

Slowly he became aware that others were up, of a town awakening to this rainstorm, and thoughts of a hot cup of coffee pushed Tyler into motion. It was still dark as the inside of a tar barrel, and he guided toward lights beaming out of a window of a building down the street. He found the building lay on a street corner, the window he came to spilling back the image of a wild, bushy-bearded derelict this rainstorm must have blown into town. Conscious for the first time in days of just how bad he looked, he brushed his hair down and stroked at his beard as he determined that the building was a mercantile store on the verge of opening for business.

"Maybe nails don't taste so bad after all . . . but coffee, got to have that . . . and maybe bum a smoke, too . . ."

The former Reb officer didn't realize that these were the same words he'd used hundreds of times in the past when times were tough and he was stone broke again. They were a habit his mind kept throwing out at him, filled as it was with failure and despair and a don't-give-a-damn-attitude. They would take him to the back doors of cafés or cheap bars or wherever he figured they needed unskilled labor to tote out slop pails or swamp up a place.

This morning those words carried Tyler across the intersection being touched by more light and along the boardwalk. His walk was steadier now, but slow and weary in the run-down boots he wore. As he moved along, he realized he was on a side street, cutting toward a ravine wall stippled with stubby pine trees. The rain didn't seem to be letting up, and he didn't care, soaked as he was getting. Even the loud crack of thunder went unnoticed as lamplight suddenly touched out of the saloon he was approaching, and then some debris mixed with sawdust billowed out of the batwings, followed by a man wielding a broom. More sawdust spilled out to splay around Tyler's legs, the man with the broom offering no apology.

"I could do that . . ."

"Yeah," grunted saloon owner Chauncey Pardee, as he kept on working the broom. Finally he stopped and took his first look at Tyler. Pardee was a wide man with his nose spread across a round face, and his head was shaved. "Mister, do you always look this bad?"

"I've had better days."

"Haven't we all?" His eyes lingered on Tyler Carradine's wet beard and choked off what he was going to say. Instead, he added, "You one of those sore-assed miners?"

"Just a drifter."

"Could use a swamper. Pay ain't all that good. You'll be takin' care of the main barroom and the back card room, and the upstairs rooms. There's a back woodshed you can bunk out in. Here"— he thrust the broom at Tyler— "finish cleanin' up the place, and we'll talk turkey about what the job pays. You just comin' off a bender?"

Tyler returned the man's cold glance. "I am. The last for me for a damned long while, though."

"Yeah, and you're broke and your belly button is raisin' hell with your backbone. There's coffee in the kitchen, and cold cuts. You might tidy up a bit, too. They call me Chaunce."

"Carradine." Broom in hand, Tyler followed after the saloon owner, passing inside along a long bar and then veering toward a pair of swinging doors. A couple of bartenders were busy restocking bottles and cleaning the bar top. He removed his wet hat and held it low at his side when they entered the large kitchen casting out a lot of heat from a black iron range presided over by a Chinaman.

"Duck Sing, just hired on a new swamper. See he's fed, and then, Carradine, start cleanin' up this place. Are you burnin' incense in here again, Sing?" His question received a vigorous smile from Sing, but he didn't push it, but swung away and left.

Staring at the newcomer, Duck Sing said scoldingly, "You stink, Mistah Callady . . ."

"Just call me Tyler. Yeah, to high heaven." He went around a chopping block and started peeling out of his outer garments by the washbasin, glad to

be in out of the rain, just damned happy that he had
a job, if only for the moment.

"Velly, velly bad hair— "

"Uh?" Swinging about, he took in Duck Sing,
standing by a chair and holding a large pair of scis-
sors.

"Snip, snip."

"Oh, you want to cut my hair? I look that bad? I
reckon so. Just a trim, dammit, and don't touch the
beard."

Only a handful of miners headed out through the
driving rainstorm for their claims, and some of these
turned back toward North Forty. Still slogging on
over the muddied trail was Henry Atwood, laden
down with a gunny sack holding food supplies. Rivu-
lets of water gouged holes in the trail and went
downslope even more to spill into swollen Mineral
Creek. He didn't mind the rain, since it would dis-
lodge old ground and stir up more pay dirt, and
most of all, he liked getting out of Jax Faraday's helltown.

The trail was crude and narrow and passed
through trees bowed some from the rain, the sky
above gray as the underbelly of a bobcat, but there
were signs where it was clearing. Even so, this would
be a good chance to sack in until it dried up right
and proper.

Engrossed in all the violence and greed he'd seen
back in town, Henry Atwood failed to see a protruding root where it snaked across the trail, and when
the toe of his muddy boot punched into it, it threw
him forward and downslope toward the stream, and
with the miner cursing at his carelessness. He hit
into wet underbrush, items from his sack spilling

around him, and then on his belly he was staring in alarm at the limp form of a dead man.

Instinctively he scrambled away, though he held there and took the time to stare into the face of sodbuster Ivan Drury. The body didn't stink, so he knew it was a recent killing. He cursed out, "These damned road agents! Nobody's safe around here."

Now caution flooded into Henry Atwood's mind, in that this was something he didn't want to be involved in. So he set about quickly gathering up his food, and then, dragging his sack, he worked his way out of the underbrush up to the trail, where he held while breathing heavily. Indecision flickered across his face. Should he head for camp, or return to North Forty?

"Nope, somebody's got to be told . . . and somebody's got to stand up against all of this villainy . . . or next time it'll be Wilbur, or me . . ."

For a man his age, and despite the years of abuse to his body, Tyler Carradine was in good shape. But even he didn't realize just how big a chore swamping out the saloon and its upstairs rooms was turning out to be. Sweat was rolling off his face and from under his clothes when he straightened up from mopping the upstairs hallway to rest his back. One of the bar girls sauntered disinterestedly by the new swamper and went clattering down the winding staircase as Tyler took in late-afternoon sunlight piercing the window at the end of the hallway.

The Chinese cook had done a workaday job on Tyler's hair, and he'd even trimmed the beard a little. At noon Tyler had returned to the kitchen, where he and Duck Sing had sat down to eat together, both social outcasts, in a way. What they had wasn't the regular fare, but some tantalizing Chinese dish. As they ate, he could feel Sing's silent eyes play over the face of the man opposite. They talked— mostly, Duck Sing did, in his singsong voice, in an attempt to put Tyler at ease.

Now he smiled in the knowledge he'd found a friendly face in a prairie of hostility. And there was Virg Tugwater, too: the farrier. Chances were, though, that Tugwater would move on, as he'd promised— that is, if that waitress didn't make her move on Tugwater.

Around him the upstairs rooms were stirring, while the rainstorm had brought in an afternoon crowd. He picked up the bucket of water and carried it out onto the back porch, emptying the bucket under the glare of a lowering sun. He didn't know what he'd be paid as a daily wage, but gauging his own opinions about the saloon owner, and what Duck Sing had told him, he wouldn't be cheated.

Wrung out from the day's work, he eased down the back staircase with the intention of checking out his sleeping quarters. To Tyler's surprise, when he pushed into the shed, his coat and hat were there, hanging from a wall peg, as well as the neat arrangement of a cot and an old rocking chair, and he knew that at least Duck Sing approved of him. But more surprising were the old but clean workworn clothes laid out on the cot.

"That old Chinaman . . . man's got a heart of gold . . ."

Right then Tyler knew it had just been pure luck, his stumbling upon this job. As he began to unbutton his shirt, Sing appeared in the doorway, gesturing that he'd pick up the other clothing, which he did. Ty followed Sing through a back door of the saloon and into a large bathroom. Sing smiled at the galvanized bathtub filled with steaming hot water. "You must wash the stink away, Callady, before we sit down for supper." And Sing left.

Later on, Tyler, feeling more relaxed in clean clothing, went up the dark hallway and at its upper end checked out the action in the gaming room. There was always the dreaded possibility he might encounter a face from the past. For the most part, the patrons were miners and whores, and a few businessmen and gamblers. Under the shading brim of his old hat, tugged kind of low over his forehead, he eased through the room while looking for Chauncey Pardee, to brace the man about his daily wage.

"Found another body," spoke out a man seated at one of the poker tables.

"I heard up around Mineral Creek . . ."

A man seated at another table joined in, "Knew him . . . some sodbuster name of Ivan Drury—"

The news of this sledgehammered at Tyler, and he turned and headed for the back hallway. *Poor Anna . . . first she gets burned out . . . now her husband has been bushwhacked. Maybe, though, she'll never find out what happened to him. Probably better that way.* She could even be coming here, he realized, in search of Ivan Drury. Since he had failed her before, Ty didn't want to confront the woman.

Now his steps carried him into the kitchen and to a small table at which he slumped down. Dropping his hat on the floor, he folded his callused hands, thoughts of Anna fading away to be replaced by a name he hadn't drummed up in years— MaryAnn. Why at this particular time should she ebb out of the dark edges of his memory? He thought about his mother, much older now and probably dead, and no doubt MaryAnn got married and had some children.

"Here . . . coffee." Duck Sing scowled down at Tyler. "You look sadder than usual, Callady . . ."

Around a grimacing smile, Tyler replied, "Nothing I can't handle. At least that rainstorm cleaned up the air."

"You smell a lot better, too."

"That's no lie. And it's Car-ra-dine."

"Okay, Callady, if you say so."

EIGHT

Weathering out last night's rainstorm under sheltering pines had given Anna Drury a chance to sort out her thoughts about the owner of the Box 7, Carl Moore, and just what to do when she got to North Forty. One thing she'd found while rummaging through the saddlebags had been a spare gunbelt containing a .32 Smith & Wesson, which she now had strapped around her slender waist. The brand on the horse she rode was unknown to Anna. *Probably stolen, like this worn saddle. First thing to do when I reach town is find Ivan . . . and then peel the hide off that no-account . . .*

She was riding along the main road, sighting in on columns of smoke pushing over an elevation beyond which rose the Wind Rivers. It was pretty damned obvious to Anna that her husband had sold out to the Faraday faction . . . something she was powerless to do anything about, though she had ideas in this direction.

Coming over a rise, with the early morning sun warming at her back, Anna got her first glimpse of the narrow draw in which North Forty was located. As she kept pressing on in, the only traveler on the road, she could see how the buildings were wedged in close along Main Street, other wooden buildings tiering up to either side. The town sure enough was out of the wind, she figured. But if a bad winter storm struck in there, the whole place would be buried to its rafters. *Gold fever brought them in . . . sucked Ivan in, too, for that matter.*

On the muddy street, the bronc walked along under slack reins. Anna checked out the signs attached to false-fronted buildings. She spotted a sign that interested her and reined thataway, saying to herself, "That rancher told me about the *Mineral Tribune* making him out as some killin' land baron. And a light is showing."

Tying up at the hitching rack, Anna held there while tucking in her woolen shirt a little and adjusted the gunbelt, though she felt awkward about this. A few people were on the street, mostly to the west, along with the Red & White Café's beckoning sign. The front door of the small building was ajar, Anna found, and she stepped inside onto a hardwood floor. Before her stood a long counter on which were scattered paper items and a stack of newspapers. Then Anna picked up on the sound of snoring, and in the back shadows, next to the printing press, she gazed at the man slumped in a rocking chair.

Moving up to the counter, she picked up the top newspaper to have the headline scream out at her: *Homesteader Murdered at the Hands of the Box 7.* Below this the main article told of how sodbuster Ivan Drury had been spirited out of North Forty by some of Carl J. Moore's killing cowpunchers and left dead along Mineral Creek. Stunned by what she was reading, and by the fact that her husband was dead, Anna felt her legs go weak, but only for a moment, since she realized this whole story was a total lie. Strangely enough, she felt no remorse over the fact Ivan was dead; theirs really had been a marriage of convenience. Softly, bitterly, she said, "He knew the risks involved in coming here. But"— her right hand stabbed the Smith & Wesson out of its holster— "this newspaper publisher is alive and knows the truth behind this."

Easing around the counter, she passed by a table covered with odds and ends, and it was here she spotted the empty whiskey bottles on the floor near the rocking chair. *Probably,* she thought disgustedly, *too drunk to tell me anything.* Though this didn't stop her from thumbing the hammer back and punching a bullet into the floor between the man's outstretched legs and awful close to his right shoe.

"What the . . ." Philo Telerude was nearsighted, and he wasn't wearing his bifocals, so all he could make out through his confusion was what appeared to be the silhouette of a cowhand. His blue-veined and heavily jowled face quivered with the shock of having been awakened. Before it could register that the intruder was a woman, Anna was in behind the man and had pressed the barrel of her gun to the nape of his neck.

In a lowered voice she whispered for him to sit still. She listened to outside sounds. When she was satisfied nobody was coming to investigate the shot, she jabbed the gun harder into his fat neck. "Please," he quavered out, "don't kill me. The cash till's up front . . . under the counter . . ."

Still masking her voice, Anna asked, "Is it true Jax Faraday owns this newspaper? No lies, or you die."

"Oh, yes, yes. I took over last month. Please, I've a wife and five kids back in Akron . . ."

Anna grimaced at this, thinking that he was just another drifting newspaperman, and a drunk, like most of them. They lasted in one place for a short while, then sought out a different locale and held in until they were no longer welcome. "That story about the killing of this sodbuster, it claims the Box 7 is behind it. I say it was Faraday or his men that killed Ivan Drury!"

"Please," he said, "I was told to print it that way."

"What about these other stories about Carl Moore and his Box 7? Are they a pack of lies, too?"

"I don't know," he wailed, his bladder all swelled up with booze and him with a cold driving fear. For all he knew, this could be C. J. Moore himself, come to kill him and Faraday. Telerude's bladder failed him.

Anna picked up on a dribbling sound and she shook her head in disgust as piss splattered onto her boots. "Oh, shit," she spat out. "Dammit, where's the coroner's office?"

"Other end of town," he wailed through his drunken throes and shame of the moment.

"Fine." Reversing her hold on the revolver, Anna swung it down hard on his head and the printer slumped in the rocking chair, though the trickling sound went on unabated. Anna Drury hurried to get away from the embarrassing situation.

Aboard her horse, she swung it to the west, her Smith & Wesson back in its holster. There was more activity on the street. She weaved her way through. The Carousel Emporium caught her eye, especially since it was the most imposing building in North Forty. "Built on the blood of others," she said with a vicious coldness.

She remembered what Carl Moore had told her, that so many had found unmarked graves around this small town. The place didn't even have a town marshal, nor a judge, just Jax Faraday as mayor, and with the authority to rule as he saw fit. Her eyes played over some hardcases lounging under the shadowing veranda on long benches.

On the ride here, and after her talk with the rancher, Anna had decided to go undercover by not revealing who she was, and to do so, she might have to get a job at Faraday's gaming salon, maybe even shine up to the slimy bastard. She doubted those men who'd set fire to her barn would recognize her, since all of that had happened before first light. Anyway, it was a chance she was more than willing to take.

The undertaker, as she now found, conducted his burying business out of a furniture store he owned—Hadley's, Inc. There were two short staircases running up onto a wide porch and some furniture on display in the front windows. Inside, Anna found there weren't any other customers, and just one clerk, who pointed her toward a curtained alcove. The long building was narrow and high-ceilinged and smelled of new furniture, the odor of formaldehyde and blood getting stronger once she was past the curtain and going with some trepidation into the preparation room.

Here she found the undertaker going over papers at a corner desk as her somber eyes played over an open pine box holding a body. She moved closer and stood there staring down at her dead husband. Ivan's hair was combed carelessly, or this could be due to the entry hole in his skull caused by a leaden slug.

"Ah . . . I didn't see you come in . . ." The undertaker rose and moved in on Anna in a calculating way. "Are you related to the deceased?"

Gazing at the man, she took in the way his nose crinkled as if smelling out newly minted double eagles, and stonily she said, "Just a friend. They say Mister Drury was murdered—"

"So I was told. Happens a lot around here."

"Which pleases you mightily, I suppose. Are church services scheduled before burial?"

Indelicately, and as if knowing she would be unprofitable to him, the undertaker said tautly, "We have no church in North Forty. I expect he'll be laid to rest this afternoon, early, as I've got other business to tend to." Rudely he turned away and sought the privacy of his desk.

Anna Drury let herself out the front door. Moving in on her horse, she found upon reaching for the saddlehorn her hand was trembling from the emotion of seeing Ivan. She let herself go all steely, though her eyes were misting a little. Once she was in the saddle, she reined out into the road, searching for a livery stable, which she chanced upon on a side street.

Walking her horse in, she took in through the open back doors a man shoeing a horse as the hostler appeared. "Got a coupla empty stalls. Or do you want to sell that horse?"

"Haven't decided yet. How are you charging?"

"Quarter a night, which includes sweet feed."

Knowing the prices were probably higher at other livery stables, Anna nodded her agreement and brought the horse into an empty stall. As she set about unsaddling it, she gazed across the center aisle at the horses tethered in stalls. Something about that grulla held her eyes, with Anna letting the cinch drop and crossing over. *Sure enough, it's the horse that damned Carradine took. So he made it here. I'd sure like to run into him. Make him admit he's working for Faraday . . .*

Grimly she went back to finish unsaddling her horse. And when this was done, she went up to be accosted by the hostler. Paying him, she asked, "Does this metropolis have any hotels or clothing stores?"

"Got some of both. Appears you're a ranchwoman . . ."

"Appears you're awful nosy. And make sure my horse gets curried." To get her point across, Anna patted the butt of her holstered revolver. "Savvy?"

NINE

In the first few days after Anna Drury had come to North Forty, two men were murdered and the usual amount of petty thievery and holdups went on, and the gamblers working at Jax Faraday's Carousel Emporium and the other gaming joints he had interests in kept up their brand of crooked dealing. This didn't seem to deter the miners from coming and bucking the games.

If anything right about now, Jax Faraday wasn't a happy man. His slanderous stories about rancher Carl Moore in the *Mineral Tribune* went unchallenged. And this worried tinhorn Faraday. So he'd called a council of war with his top hardcases, Robinson and Rafe Belsing, and Carney Aker.

"You're crazy, we just can't up and bushwhack C. J. Moore!"

"At least he'd be out of your hair."

"And we'd have federal marshals pouring in here," Faraday chided Carney Aker. "Need I remind everyone there's a fine line between respectability and a federal pen?"

"He'll crack," muttered Harney Robinson. "They all do." For some eerie reason he couldn't plumb, in him had arisen a name out of his Civil War past— Tyler Carradine. And why now? For years he hadn't even looked southeasterly to that bloody conflict. It could be, though he seriously doubted it, turncoat Carradine was still alive, and maybe in these parts. Or even here in North Forty. If so, he'd damn well finish the job by executing the son'bitch.

"You've got something in mind, Harney?"

He let whiskey gurgle into his glass. He sat with the other hardcases while Jax Faraday was pacing his office like an angry mountain lion. "That plat map over there, Jax, shows one prime piece of real estate; smack dab along Sandy Creek, an' right in betwixt your land and that of the Box 7. Homestead is owned by a man named Rickart, just him and his half-witted son."

He knew that the foxy Harney Robinson wouldn't be telling him about some sodbuster unless all the facts about the man were in, and he stopped pacing and said, "I expect this'll cost me."

"After you hear me out, Jax, I reckon both of us will profit out of this. I doubt if any one Box 7 hand, much less Moore himself, has ever laid eyes on this sodbuster. You ever hear of Pops Levansky?"

"Go on," Faraday said from the side bar.

"Pops just blew into town, bib overalls and all. Anyway, every vice squad detective from the Bronx to New Orleans knows Pops Levansky. A true con artist if ever there was one. The first thing is to get that sodbuster out of the way. Then Pops'll head over to Big Sandy, as that's where the Box 7 buys their supplies."

"With intentions of selling his homestead to Carl Moore— "

"Yup, that covers it, Jax. The trick is to have Pops head back to his place, instead of hangin' around Big Sandy, waitin' for Moore to show. Fast as a hunk of pork passes through a goose, that rancher'll be beelinin' over to buy out Pops Levansky. Moore'll get

there, awright, and when he does, he gets gunned
down from ambush."

"Well, it sounds good . . . but . . ."

"You're thinkin' the only loophole is Pops Levansky. Don't worry, I've got that covered, too."

"I like the idea, Harney, of this thing taking place
a long ways from North Forty." Now he told Belsing
and Aker to leave. Faraday settled down on the edge
of his desk. "The next is for your ears only, Harney.
The word I got is that a couple of U.S. marshals are
due to arrive. I expect this is the handiwork of Carl
Moore. Pass the word that for the next few weeks
there'll be no more strong-arm stuff."

"The boys won't like it."

"It isn't these bloodthirsty hardcases I'm worried
about," retorted Faraday. "Meanwhile, I want to see
this Pops Levansky. What is he, some misplaced
Okie?"

"No tellin' what rock Pops crawled out from under.
But he's about the best scam artist around."

"Seeing how damned cautious you are, Harney, I'll
agree with this. What we don't want to do is to rush
into this . . . lay it out awful careful-like. Okay, now
let's do some money talk."

Now that night was settling in on North Forty as
if it weighed more than the day, hardcase Carney
Aker felt a lot easier. He hated just getting up in the
morning or being out in the sun too long, but come
nightfall, Aker was in his element. He rarely hit the
sack before four or five in the morning. And now
that he was being paid regularly, he generally shared
his bed with some whore.

He had no particular loyalty toward Jax Faraday,
other than that it gave Aker a chance to use his

shootin' iron when someone displeased him. His hair trigger was the chief reason murder warrants were out on him in Texas and the Nations, as they were on his riding partner, Rafe Belsing. Neither of them had much use for the ambitious Harney Robinson, nor for the fat bastard's mean mouth. If it ever came down to it, to leaving, Aker had vowed he'd gun down Harney.

"Dammit, Rafe, I just don't like it the way Faraday kicked us out of his office."

"Man's an uppity dipshit, awright. Leave it be. Look at all these women prancin' about . . ."

"The new one sure keeps givin' me the eye. Said her name was Anna something."

"Yeah?" Belsing questioned. His indifferent gaze took in Anna Drury carrying a pitcher of beer over to a table. He didn't figure her as being all that pretty. She'd started working, what, a week ago now? Whatever, and if the opium or rotgut didn't do her in, she'd succumb to some other vice. The odds were stacked against her, and every bar girl and whore, and even him, he knew. A sidelong glance took in Carney Aker, sitting a little slumped under the load of all the whiskey he'd put away. Lately, he was thinking hard that Carney was expendable, and worse, too dependent on him when the chips were down. But habits, even bad ones, were hard to break.

He tossed a cigar Aker's way. "Drag on that, Carney. Yeah, she ain't all that bad. You figurin' on holdin' in here, I reckon, so I'm drifting out to try my luck over at the Palace."

"Sure, Rafe, catch you later."

"That'll be breakfast you're springin' for."

Returning the smile of the miner who'd just paid her for the pitcher of beer, Anna Drury saw to her satisfaction that Rafe Belsing had just left. The easiest part had been getting a job as a barmaid. Learning the ropes here at Faraday's casino meant being manhandled by this seedy lot of drifters and tinhorns. And playing up to Carney Aker, a man she despised. In his cups, Aker would open up and tell her all kinds of unsavory things, a lot of it half-truths. But a pattern was emerging that she hoped would take her right to Jax Faraday.

The dark red dress she wore showed plenty of cleavage, though Anna's makeup was a mask behind which she hid her true feelings. She had no sympathy for the miners coming in here and getting fleeced. It was her notion they ought to know better. Her deceased husband had the same character flaws.

Around midnight and on until three o'clock it was an elbow-to-elbow crowd, and she was hard pressed to keep up with her drink orders, something that helped to take her mind off why she was here in the first place. Her eyes were smarting from the thick pall of smoke, even though the doors and some of the windows were open. The noise was just as thick, and to Anna, an annoying babble she simply ignored. Turning away from the bar at an irritated request for another drink, she bumped into Carney Aker, grinning at her through lust-filled eyes.

"Excuse me . . ."

"Hey, about time we cut out of here, darlin'."

"If I did, I'd get fired."

"Yeah, I can fix that." Rudely he brushed by her and went behind the bar and accosted the head bartender. "Me an' her are leavin' . . . any arguments, Baxter?"

"No . . . nope, Mister Aker. You go right away. G'night, Anna."

Now Anna Drury went ahead of the drunken hardcase to find a back hallway and her coat and handbag in one of the storerooms. Along with a derringer, her handbag had in it a pint bottle of corn liquor into which she'd mixed knockout drops. They went out a back door, with Carney Aker laying a heavy arm over her shoulder and reeling as he walked, and chattering away.

"That Harney Robinson is gettin' too uppity," he groused, as he brought her onto a side street and toward his hotel. "We was up in Faraday's office . . . an' it was Harney this an' Harney that about a plan of his to . . ." He pulled up short and gazed across the dirt street at Chauncey Pardee's Golden Steer bar. Sometimes he would accompany the bossman over here, Faraday, who'd then receive an envelope containing protection money. Everyone paid, or they didn't last long in North Forty. Licking out his tongue at his stubbled chin in thoughtful contemplation, there came a spear of resentment. Here he was, about busted, and right across the street was easy pickings. "Come on, doll, just the place for us to get some free drinks and a fistful of dollars."

He half fell, and Anna had to help the hardcase regain his footing, and with Aker laughing at this. Then he was blundering in first, the batwings springing back to be caught by Anna, who held there as the hardcase surveyed what was left of tonight's crowd. Around a dozen hunkered in quietly at two poker tables. Even their cigar and handrolled smoke, which hung heavy in lazy patterns above them, seemed to be frozen in weariness, like the players waiting for first light, when maybe the game would end. Early on, though Aker didn't know this, there'd been a knifing, a common enough malady among rough men, and the bartenders eyeing the drunken hardcase heading their way were awful leery. As they knew who Carney Aker worked for.

"What'll it be, Carney?"

"Me an' my lady friend . . ." He pirouetted drunkenly around and gestured impatiently for Anna to join him at the bar. "Ain't she the shy one, though?" His guffawed laughter cut through the silence. He had the bar cowed and was enjoying it, a hard, challenging glint in his eyes for the poker players. The bartender had only placed one shot glass on the bar top, to have Aker snap out, "You lost your manners? Another glass . . . and that better be top shelf . . ."

"Please, Carney, these men have probably worked all night." Through the sweet, pleading tone of Anna's voice, her eyes were shuddering with concealed anger. "I . . . really I don't care for anything to drink . . ."

"Suit yourself," grinned Aker, as he downed his and set it down to have the bartender slop in more whiskey. "Mister Faraday sent me over to pick up the protection money."

"I, ah, Chauncey always handles that— "

"Now. I want the money *now*," the hardcase countered, drawing and pointing his six-shooter at the bartender scuttling around and picking up the cash box. "How . . . how much is it, Mister Aker?"

"Here, put the damn box on the bar. Okay, that's better." He shot a wink at Anna upon leathering his gun and then began picking up folding money and double eagles and stuffing everything into his coat pockets. He knew another cash box contained gold dust and nuggets, but what he had, he decided, was enough for tonight. "Obliged." This was said through a burp, and he grasped Anna's arm and led her outside, to continue on along to Aker's hotel.

Back in the saloon, the head bartender was shooting curses after the hardcase, knowing that he'd better wake up Chauncey Pardee and tell the man he worked for what had happened. There was also scattered talk about this from the tables. It soon died away when the players got down to the business of poker.

Neither the players nor the bartenders had noticed the silent witness holding back in the gloomy shadows, the man there still not believing he'd been looking at Anna Drury. "At least she's alive," Tyler Carradine said to the shadows hemming him in.

Only because he couldn't sleep had Tyler gotten up earlier than usual. In about an hour he would start the tedious process of cleaning up the Golden Steer. In the kitchen he'd warmed up a cold pot of coffee and brought it and a cup out here to watch the card players. He didn't know any of them and could care less who lost heavily. But he did care about one thing, and that was that Anna Drury hadn't spotted him.

Can't help it she got burned out. Too far away for me to make any difference about that. She's alive . . . and here. But does she know that her husband has been killed? This was something that had slipped Tyler's mind until now, and he was tempted to go after her. *No,* came the voice of indifference, *don't mess into this, as she'll soon find out about it.*

He couldn't help noticing how boldly she was dressed, and being with that hardcase meant to Tyler that she probably had hired on at Faraday's place. She sure seemed different from the Anna he had briefly known during that one long night. Damn, she'd been there for him, a bulwark of strength when he had told some of his past and his reasons for running, always running. With an abruptness, Tyler rose and took the cup and pot back into the kitchen, discarding any thoughts of Anna, or anything else, for that matter.

* * *

Down a block, Anna Drury was finding that Aker could barely make it up the staircase. He'd told her his room number, and soon they were inside the room, where she let Aker flop, grinning, onto the narrow bed. He kept on directing words at her, with Anna always steering his mind to Jax Faraday. "You were telling me about this plan of Harney's . . ."

"Yup, about what this windbag claims he can do. Hey, that a pint of whiskey you brung along, doll?"

"Go on about Harney first."

"Damn fool has come up with a plan to take out this rancher, Carl Moore. Harney spoke about some con artist, Pops somethin'-or-other . . . but to hell with that blowhard. Just plant your sweet little behind down next to me." At this he was handed the pint bottle, from which he gurgled down more whiskey like a man dried out by the sun and wind. "Like I said . . . I . . . goin' kind of fuzzy in here . . ."

"You shouldn't drink so much," she scolded Aker, who was going suddenly limp. "Better yet, you killin' an' thievin' bastard, keep drinkin' until your kidneys give way."

Now Anna found she had to lean against the wall by the door, her boldness gone for the moment and a lassitude gripping her legs. She knew that Aker would sleep on through most of tomorrow, and anyway, nobody would miss the braggart. Through the east window, she realized, pale light was filtering in past the yellowed-out curtains. She was plumb worn out. "Harney Robinson has this plan . . . involving some con man named Pops. If they do kill Carl Moore, Faraday's brand of law will spread all over the basin like the plague. But first, there's all this money Aker helped himself to."

Returning to the bed, she managed to pry his left coat lapel away from his inert form and get her hands into one of the side pockets. She filled her small purse with silvery coin and some of the greenbacks. This would be a nest egg against her being found out by Faraday or his men. She couldn't help noticing this town had a few down-and-outers. *Like Tyler Carradine. Mentioned his name to Aker the other day . . . and drew a blank. But I know Carradine is here someplace. You were a fool, girl, for letting him share your bed. More of a fool to marry Ivan Drury.*

Now Anna Drury left the room to go boldly, tiredly, down the front staircase and out into the street. As she passed the Golden Steer Saloon, a sidelong glance would have revealed Tyler Carradine holding one of the batwing doors open as he plied his broom. Instead Anna's thoughts were astir with all she'd learned tonight.

TEN

That night, in the solitude of his bunk, sleep kept eluding Tyler Carradine. There was nothing unusual about this, except that tonight, for a change, he was cold sober, and in this condition a lot of unwanted thoughts kept spinning about, most of them about Anna Drury.

She didn't seem the sort to cast her lot with that sorry bunch over at the Carousel Emporium, unless those who'd burned her out had been from the Box 7. Somehow, this didn't set right, either, as Tyler had picked up on bar talk which painted a different picture of rancher Carl J. Moore than the versions of the man appearing in Faraday's ragsheet of a newspaper. *Only Anna Drury knows what happened out there. But not what happened to her husband. Since nothing about his death was written up in the* Tribune. *An' I reckon by order of Jax Faraday.*

Through a bitter and regretful sigh Tyler suddenly pushed up from his bunk, as he felt a driving need to see Anna again. It was something he couldn't explain, a feeling, maybe, out of the past, of the time when his whole being had been centered on another woman. Or was it because he felt so lonely, filled with a craving to catch a glimpse of Anna's face again and that wonderful smile?

Last night, in the Golden Steer, when Anna and

that hardcase had dropped in, it wasn't so much the shock of seeing her, but that hard set to her face, and in a way, her guarded body language. This alone told him she was involved in some deadly game. Now he found himself tucking his long-sleeved shirt into a fairly new pair of Levis. The old boots were gone too, the hat Tyler adjusted over his trimmed brown hair still retaining its low-crowned shape, though he still wore his beard fairly thick. He ducked a little to clear the low door frame and came out of the shed into a pleasantly warm night, embracing the lights and sounds of North Forty.

Purposely Tyler kept to the alleyway running behind the saloon and other business places, a habit that was hard to break. Even at night he felt uneasy about encountering anyone and their inquiring eyes when they saw his face. On Main Street, he paused by a hardware store shuttered down for the night and regarded all that he saw in the way of traffic and lights haloing away from the saloons. He wasn't packing a gun and saw no need for it, since at the first sign of trouble he would peel away and find a more safe place.

His attention went west three blocks to the spacious white painted casino where he knew Faraday would be, and some of his gunslicks, and possibly Anna. He'd never set foot in the place, and apprehension settled in as he stepped along. He picked out faces of passersby who frequented Chauncey Pardee's saloon, although none of them recognized Tyler in his neater attire.

A wagon with a yonker handling the reins swung in toward Tyler just as he left the boardwalk and came into the intersection, the eyes of the pair of horses wide and rolling and the team about to run away as if sensing the yonker's fear and inexperience.

One of the horses reared, and almost as if it were someone else, Tyler found himself breaking over to grab the halter of the other horse and hang on tight, managing to bring the wagon to a halt.

"Easy." He patted the horse's forehead, calm and not at all worked up over what had just happened, and was kind of surprised he could still think on his feet. He went back and smiled at the kid of fourteen who'd managed to throw the hand brake.

"Thanks, mister."

"No problem. You going far?"

"Outskirts of town, I hope. Thanks again."

Nodding, Tyler stepped past the wagon to suddenly bump into a pair of women moving in the same direction it appeared. And he blurted out, "Sorry, ladies, I . . ."

"Carradine?"

"Anna . . . I . . ." Panic set into Tyler's mind like a fused stick of dynamite. "I . . . nothing. I . . ." Instinct to get away from any further involvement, something he couldn't explain, caused Tyler to break into a run back along his backtrail.

"Carradine, dammit, I want to talk to you!"

He swung back and shouted at Anna Drury, "Got to tell you, Anna, your husband . . . he's dead . . ." The next moment he was pushing down a narrow opening between two buildings and heading for a back street, and from here, the Golden Steer Saloon. He needed a drink bad after this. He owed the woman nothing other than telling her about her husband. Now he groaned out, "Damn you, Carradine, you're a miserable coward . . . always runnin' away. Maybe before long there'll be no more places to run to, to hide out in. . . ."

* * *

"What was that all about?"

"I don't rightly know," said Anna in a puzzling voice to her woman companion. "Ran like he was about to be tarred and feathered." The remembrance of the night Tyler Carradine had spent at her log cabin brought further revelations of what he'd told her about his past. It seemed Tyler feared confrontation on any level, but that he was actually here in North Forty only firmed up Anna's reasons for wanting to corral him and get to the bottom of this. She hadn't seen him hanging around Faraday's place, a good sign. Meaning he must have been just that, a saddle tramp ghosting through the basin.

And over at the Carousel Emporium, and at a table reserved for men with money, Harney Robinson was hunkered in close to a silver-haired man with leonine features. The woolen shirt worn by Pops Levansky was buttoned at the collar and it was large, as were the bib overalls he had on. It appeared Levansky wasn't packing a gun, when in fact he had a small pistol tucked in one of his boots and another in the checkered coat he'd duffed. His facial skin was smooth. He had big red cheekbones and luminous blue eyes under white shaggy brows. The con man was in his middle sixties and in deceptively good shape, but even so, Pops didn't exactly cotton to playing the role of sodbuster, or that long horseback ride over to Big Sandy. Especially when here in North Forty there was plenty of action for a man of his trade.

"You always held onto a hole card, Harney," he said.

"You're right, Pops, I haven't told you all of it. Just the part about getting rid of that meddling rancher. And you're right, too, a lot of things could go wrong." His raised arm brought a bar girl over with another bottle of whiskey. "This whole thing shouldn't take more'n a week. Leave hog-tying that

sodbuster and his son up to Rafe Belsing; Rafe's as
hard as they come, an' he'll do what I say."

"Yes, I can see your reasons, Harney, for keeping
them alive. You have quite a town here . . . quite an
expensive place to hang out in . . ."

Harney Robinson grinned back at the con man. "I
could give you part of your fee in prime land, Pops.
But you're a drifter, so instead, just how much more
do you want?"

"If I were really interested . . ."

"I know you're hooked on this."

"Flimflamming that rancher has a certain appeal.
You add another two thousand, Mister Robinson, and
I shall indeed suffer the agonies of a long ride on
some addled bronc."

"Seven thousand's a heap, Pops. I'll have to chew it
over with Faraday, as he's handling the purse strings.
Meanwhile, here's that thousand I promised you in
earnest money." He emptied his shot glass around an
impatient grimace. "Got to make the rounds with
Faraday, as it's collection night. Should have some of
his strong-arms handle it, but he don't trust them,
either. I'll be back around midnight or so, with Faraday's answer."

As Robinson took to the staircase on his way up to
Jax Faraday's office, Anna Drury kept watching the
man who'd shared Robinson's table while coming in
on a table with a tray of fresh drinks. It could be
just another homesteader in here, hoping to sell out.
She wanted to go over and warn the gray-haired man
but was held back from this by an inner caution. Col-
lecting for the drinks, along with getting a pat on
her thigh from a drunken miner, she shook her head
at the sight of Pops Levansky sitting in on a poker
game. *Something about that old geezer bothers me. Must
have sold out, as he's flashing a hefty roll. Leave it be.*

Tonight, if what Carney Aker had told her was true, Faraday would be going out to make some collections. Something about protection insurance, a strong-arm tactic used back East, she recalled, by gangsters. And when Faraday was doing this, she hoped to gain access to his office.

"Hey, missy, over here."

"Yeah, I hear you." Anna smiled below her guarded eyes.

Others had also been holding out here in Faraday's gaming hall in the form of two men sitting quietly at a wall table. Harney Robinson's going upstairs had been a signal for one of these men to slip out the back door. The other man in his disguise as a miner held to the table while sipping occasionally from a glass of warm beer. He had a narrow, high-cheeked face burned by the weather, and until two weeks ago, he'd been hunting for rustlers down in southwestern Wyoming.

The first telegram out of the U.S. marshal's office in Cheyenne had caught up with Troy Burch in the railroad town of Green River. Then an exchange of more wires had filled him and deputy marshal Hogan Fuller in as to the situation over here at North Forty. Burch had deliberately avoided letting anyone, even the complainant in this case, basin rancher C. J. Moore, know they were here. In this business you learned the only man you could trust was your partner. Both Burch and Hogan Fuller were in their early thirties and had been federal lawmen for nearly six years. Years that had aged the pair of them, seen Fuller divorced, seen both of them nicked by bullets. Both of them had killed in the line of duty and had learned to live with this.

You didn't have to be any too swift to know Jax Faraday's games were crooked or the whiskey was wa-

tered down until it damned near tasted like donkey
piss. There were the muggings, the occasional killing,
the obvious things everybody spoke about guard-
edly. Once you got out of North Forty, it was this
land-buying game between Faraday and the Box 7. *The
local newspaper has sure got Carl Moore buried-to his neck
in quicksand as bein' the root of all these troubles. Can't
judge, as I've never met the man, while Faraday's slick as
they come. Once we get through all that bear grease he uses
in his pomaded hair, reckon we'll come up with something.
That bar girl, now . . . this Anna . . . just doesn't fit, her
working here . . .*

Quietly, Marshal Burch had discovered that she was
the wife of recently deceased Ivan Drury and a little
about how her homestead had been sold out from
under her. When he could, he and Hogan Fuller
would head over to the county seat and check out land
records. This gold strike, they had determined, was
running out of steam. The miners would leave another ghost town in their wake, a fact that Jax Faraday
was doing something about. "Man's got to have records hidden away upstairs about all his land dealings.
Though there ain't no crime against bein' ambitious."

He kept watching Anna Drury through covert eyes,
the feeling strong in him that they would have a sit-
down talk, and damned soon. If he had picked up on
her as being up to something, others working here
probably had seen or sensed the same thing and were
probably just waiting for her to make a false move.
He didn't want her killed. It just could be she'd found
out something about Faraday. As yet, they couldn't
pin a thing on the mayor of North Forty, and this was
getting to Troy Burch. The town didn't even have a
town marshal, or city clerk or town council, a cold
turkey killin' place.

Eleven

Once hardcase Carney Aker had managed to revive from his drunken stupor and the Mickey Finn served to him by Anna Drury, naturally he had reverted to a habit older than his last coherent thought, this through gloating over his ill-gotten gains while wobbling on shaky legs over to Willi Crankscrew's Cacti Bar, a favorite watering hole.

He soon forgot all about Anna Drury when a sloe-eyed woman enticed him to one of the tables, and then the sight of all that money being spent by Carney Aker brought in other bar girls. A couple of times as the evening wended on he bought drinks, lost again in an alcoholic haze.

Across town, the man Aker worked for had a reserved smile for the man who'd just handed him an envelope containing a large sheaf of greenbacks. Quickly Jax Faraday slipped the envelope into an inner coat pocket and said, "Thanks, Mike. How's business been lately?"

"Tapering off some," the saloon owner said grudgingly. "Got my place up for sale." Though he held to the chair, he was anxious to clear away from Faraday and his pair of hardcases. Bitterly he resented having to pay this tinhorn anything, though he knew that to flare out would cost him dearly. His smile holding, he picked up the whiskey bottle and refilled the glass of Harney Robinson, seated to his right. The other hardcase, Rafe Belsing, stood off, absorbed in a game of faro. "Yup, I got a couple of offers, but nothin' concrete."

Jax Faraday took this in as he rolled a new cigar around in his long, supple fingers. What saloon owner Mike Kalinoski hadn't said in so many words was that the miners weren't finding too much gold anymore, though the pages of advertising in Faraday's newspaper were still bringing them in. So what Faraday saw was a different future for North Forty, a cowtown of some size— the railroad would see to that. In a quiet voice, he opined his feelings about this to the saloon owner. The reasoning behind this for Jax Faraday was still guarded, in that he needed some friends, since word had got to him that it could be some federal lawmen were snooping about town. Maybe a year ago he'd have said to hell with this, and hired on more gunhands.

Instead, he speared Kalinoski with a smile laced with friendliness— something that seemed out of sorts for Faraday, a man known to have a violent temper. "You know, Mike, it's no secret I've been buying land. The Great Divide Basin, they call this place . . . a place where cattle can graze and a man can be something. But we need places like North Forty. You've got salt, Mike, hate to see you pull out."

Tentatively, he responded to the friendly glint in Faraday's eyes. "Truth is, I like it out here." He left it there, aware now that something in their relationship was about to change, but still holding onto his caution. His eyes narrowed reflectively as Faraday dipped a hand inside his coat and the envelope reappeared.

"Here," Faraday said, "I'm giving back half the money. This is just between us, Mike."

"Sure, I got no problem with that."

"My men will still be around to see your property is protected. If anything, Mike, there are more knifings and the like than before. As mayor, and speaking for the other businessmen"— Faraday rose lithely— "we'd hate to have you sell out."

With a departing nod for Faraday, the saloon owner hooked a pondering hand around the empty whiskey bottle. *Bastard's tryin' to buy friends. Maybe the rumor's true there's some federal boys in town. If so, this chiseler's days could be numbered around here. I might stick around just to see Jax Faraday come tumblin' down . . .*

Finished with his business on Main Street, Jax Faraday and his men took to the bars and gaming places on the Northside. It wasn't until after one o'clock that he reached one of the last places on his list, the Golden Steer. Faraday had limited his drinking to about five jiggers of whiskey, not that he couldn't handle it, but lately, even whiskey couldn't lift him out of this surly mood brought about by his private worries.

He came in behind Robinson and Belsing, separating as they came in on the crowded bar. Their appearance, which took place only once a month, caused some of the bar patrons to step aside, and then the noise picked up as if nothing had happened. Harney Robinson cast a bored glance around at the same old faces of men in worn garb and the jaded women. The saloon owner passed under Harney's scrutinizing glance and came to stand by Faraday, close to the bar, where the pair of them took in a miner exploding in excitement when his number came up a winner on the roulette wheel.

"Mister Faraday," Pardee suggested quietly, "let's go back to my office."

Shrugging, Faraday said, "Guess I've had enough

of the same old noise myself. How's it going, Pardee?"
Trailing him were Belsing and Harney Robinson,
threading around the back tables, only to draw up
when the saloon owner revealed questioningly to Faraday that one of his men had been in a couple of days
ago.

"Aker . . . that's it, I believe it was Aker. Came in
here with some woman, as a matter of fact." Then
he laid out what took place to Jax Faraday.

Back in the kitchen, cook Duck Sing was hunkered
in over a table playing checkers with Tyler Carradine,
who'd been drinking steadily ever since stumbling
back here after running unexpectedly into Anna
Drury. Sing disapproved of what he saw, though he
wouldn't voice his opinion. As a Chinaman, he, too,
knew all about prejudice and failure, and unlike Tyler,
he hadn't given up. He had seen in recent days the
increasing signs of restlessness, which meant his
friend would disappear again. Into the kitchen came
the anger-pitched voice of Chauncey Pardee and the
voice of another man responding in kind, and Sing
half rose as he threw Tyler a questioning glance.

"It appears there's some trouble."

"I suppose," Tyler said. "None of our business."

Resentful of the tall Southerner's lack of loyalty to
the man they worked for, Duck Sing stepped cautiously out into the hallway and gazed barward at
Pardee being braced by, it seemed, three men. He
recognized Jax Faraday, and then Faraday was lashing
out at Pardee, "You don't pay anybody else, you hear,
Pardee? I don't give a damn that Carney Aker got
away with some of your money. I want mine—and
damned quick!"

"You thievin' bastard!" Chauncey Pardee exploded.
"Aker has your protection money. An' that's all you're
goin' to get, Faraday!"

Stung by the bar owner's brazen attitude, Faraday lost what little hold he had on the rest of his temper. He shoved Pardee against the nearby wall, a signal to his men to back him up, to have this followed by a backhanded blow by Faraday to Pardee's face. He was about to hit Pardee again only to hear a gun go off almost in his ear, which caused Faraday to blink in alarm.

The bullet fired from Rafe Belsing's six-shooter took the Chinaman squarely in the chest, as Duck Sing had pulled out a hideout knife and was coming to the aid of his boss, and then he was dead and crumpling down. "Got me a Chink," chortled Belsing.

At the sound of the shot, Tyler Carradine had risen to his feet just in time to see Duck Sing take a hit and go down. Just like that, something snapped in Tyler, maybe all the years of pent-up anger, for he broke out into the hallway and stepped over Sing's prone form to come in on those accosting Chauncey Pardee.

His bearded face all contorted with rage, and his hair askew, Tyler was suddenly in on Belsing still grasping his gun, and with Belsing's eyes filled with a new uncertainty. Before he could react, a sledgelike fist caught him squarely in the throat, with Belsing going loose-limbed and tumbling back over a table.

It was here that Harney Robinson took over as he shouted out, "Hold it, you stupid barfly!" Thumbing back the hammer on his drawn revolver, he added, "I oughta kill you right here, damn you!"

Still in a fighting crouch, Tyler let some of his anger flare away, common sense taking hold to tell him he was a split second from dying. And he held there, glaring at the three men. "What Pardee says is true," Tyler muttered loudly, "your man Aker claimed that money."

"I told you so," threw in Pardee.

"Shut up," snapped Harney Robinson, unable to tear his eyes away from Tyler, the drumbeat of memory tattooing away from the dark and forgotten edges of the past. He knew this man, had heard that hard Southern voice before, and it had to be someone who'd fought in the war as he'd done. "I know you . . ."

It struck out at Tyler first, to have a sick feeling punch into his stomach, along with a bitter and unforgiving anger. "You always were a lying sonofabitch! You framed me back there, back in Missouri. See these scars marking my face? They were put there when I was hog-tied in that jail . . . by Colonel Wannabey— a jinglebob spur, that's what he used. All because of your damned lies, Robinson!"

"Shit," grinned Harney Robinson, "you're nothin' but a cowardly turncoat. Sold out to the bluecoats." His grin widened when Tyler started moving toward him, and then his gun barked and the slug nicked Tyler's left forearm, drawing blood.

"Don't be foolish, Tyler," warned Chauncey Pardee. "Take another step, and this big hunk of bull blubber will kill you. Ease away, now."

Tyler did stop, and when he did, he held up a warning finger that zeroed in on Harney Robinson's ruddy face, and Tyler said icily, "I've been running all these years. From the likes of scum like you, Robinson." His voice dropped away, and he turned with complete contempt and disregard for the gun held by Harney Robinson and started up the back hallway toward the kitchen. Through his agony of the moment, Tyler crouched down and gathered Duck Sing's body into his arms and close to his chest. From here he went out the back door and made his way toward his shed.

Inside the saloon, Chauncey Pardee said coldly, "You just may have done Carradine a favor."

"He makes any trouble," said Faraday, "and he's dead." His eyes went to Rafe Belsing beginning to come around, and he snapped at Robinson, "You and Rafe, go and find that damned Carney Aker. Okay, Pardee, let's just say that you paid up a little earlier than I anticipated. But whatever Aker is short, you make up." He spun around and was soon going out the front door followed by his men.

Before this, however, Chauncey Pardee was heading toward the back door. Once he was outside, light beaming from the shed drew him there. Through the screen door he looked in at Tyler Carradine slumped on a chair by the cot on which Duck Sing was stretched out. He let himself inside. Only then did Tyler lift his head, gazing intently at Pardee, who recognized instantly the fires of revenge, like he was seeing Tyler Carradine for the first time.

"We . . . both . . . lost a good friend . . ."

"That we did," intoned Tyler, "that we did."

"I'll see Duck Sing is buried proper."

"And I aim to make amends for too many bad years, Chauncey."

"By goin' against Faraday's killers? A no-win situation."

"I trust you won't try to stop me?"

"No . . ."

"That you'll back my play?"

"Me . . . and others, Tyler, for damned sure. Robinson, you did know him from . . . before . . ."

A wicked smile lifted the corners of Tyler's wide mouth, and suddenly he felt alive, filled with a deadly purpose, and damn the consequences. "My problem was, suh, I was a proper Southerner . . . filled with pride and purpose . . . the South was all that counted." He reached over and laid a hand over Duck Sing's, folded over his stomach. "This was an honorable man. My friend. Reckon, suh, all the pride and purpose I need to do some ass kicking. Reckon, too, Chauncey, I'll be needin' a brace of shootin' irons—"

"Just happen to have a matched pair of Samuel Colt's finest."

"Obliged. I'm goin' to disappear for a few days. Out in the boonies, as I need to regain my shootin' touch."

"Place you can stay at, Tyler, out there, is up in the Wind Rivers, just an old hunting cabin. Some lakes nearby, and a lot of privacy."

Through a grieving nod, Tyler lifted the blanket and covered Duck Sing's face. He unbent from the chair and came to tower over the saloon owner. He hadn't bothered, and maybe had forgot, to tend to the slight arm wound. "When I get back, I'm a-hoping, Chauncey, we can gather some who'll stand up to Jax Faraday. But first there's Rafe Belsing . . . and . . ."

"And Harney Robinson?"

"Him, too!"

One of the first places checked out by Rafe Belsing and Harney Robinson was the Cacti Bar, and afterward they hit other places, looking for Carney Aker. They didn't have to look far. Belsing threw up a quick hand toward the man they sought stumbling out of a Main Street saloon. "Drunk, as usual. This should be easy."

"Ain't he your ridin' partner—"

"Things don't always last," muttered Belsing, the hope in him that Carney hadn't spent all that money. They were closing in quickly on Carney Aker, groping like a blind man along the front wall of a building, and when Aker stopped to relieve himself, the others stopped, too, and Belsing fished a knife out of his pocket.

Harney Robinson, his gun out and holding back a little, grunted in satisfaction when Belsing slammed the head of the man they were going to kill into the board wall. Belsing plunged the knife blade deep into the back of his victim, muttering, "Way it goes sometimes, Carney." And then Aker was sprawled dead on the hard-backed ground, with his former partner pawing eager hands through the pockets in search of money and ignoring Robinson, who'd stepped in closer.

"Half of what you find is mine, you hear, Rafe? Wish it was that bastard Carradine lyin' there."

Coming erect, the pair of them stealing away, Belsing inquired, "That crazy-lookin' swamper over at the Golden Steer . . ." He passed some of the money to Robinson. "Just go for it."

"Yup, to hell with Faraday. Catch you later."

TWELVE

A week passed, some rain hitting into the basin, more of it along Sandy Creek, where Rafe Belsing and two other gunhands sat wetly aboard their horses while taking in a cabin hugging into the side of a hill. With them was con man Pops Levansky, from the bitter set to his face, wishing he had spurned this job.

"A man named Rickart and his son."

"They must be in there."

"Yeah," Belsing said darkly, as he told one of his men to ride up and get onto the roof. "Just sling your rain slicker over that stovepipe." He drew his six-gun and rode in along the rocky bank toward the front of the cabin, impatient to get this over with as he wanted to get in there and dry out. They'd decided to try and take the homesteaders alive and would kill them later when that rancher showed up. Now the others reined in to either side, just as antsy as Belsing to get in there.

In a couple of minutes, first one, then the other homesteader stumbled, gagging, out the front door, with Belsing tempted to take them out. He didn't particularly like keeping them alive, and instead he threw out, "Hog-tie them and throw them in that shed. Damn rain, anyway."

The rain let up a day later, which brought Pops

Levansky on the move along an old trail for the basin cowtown of Big Sandy. He arrived in the early evening and stabled his horse before securing a room at the only hotel.

In the days that followed, he simply loafed around town, letting it be known he was sure hoping some Box 7 hands or even Carl Moore would ride into town, as Levansky wanted to unload at any price his forlorn homestead out along Sandy Creek. Since he'd found out that the hands from the Box 7 hung out at Gurney's Mad-Dog Bar, one of three saloons in Big Sandy, the con man did likewise, playing penny ante poker and grudgingly forking over a worn nickel for a stein of beer. In his bib overalls and woolen shirt frayed at the elbows, he looked worse for wear than the other players, and they accepted Pops Levansky at face value.

Tonight the saloon was operating under the glare of new lamps and reflector lights, and everyone was commenting about this, since the owner of the place was awful tight with his money. One wag was damned sure this might even make the front page of the North Forty *Tribune* or the *Star*, a Casper newspaper sadly lacking in imagination.

Another player at Levansky's table grumbled over sad eyes, and as he folded his hand, he said, "Son-'bitch is gonna raise prices in here, I just know it."

"Ah, shit, Barney, you'd bitch if they hung you with a new rope. I see you're foldin', too, Eldon."

"You raisin', Toby, or what?"

This impatient retort came from local banker Ben-Lee Pentecost, a wizened man with walnut-colored skin pinched tight to the bone of his small face. He had his chair tucked in closer to the table than the others as he wasn't more than five feet tall. By reputation he was a man who could rattle off addin' up figures faster than a cockroach could scurry down the saloon's nicked bar, a hazardous journey, since basin cowhands liked to unlimber their shootin' irons to hurry the long-limbed bug along. Banker Pentecost, though he sat into high-stakes games, liked to come in here and take small change from men he wouldn't invite to his house.

Gents that've never even seen the inside of his bank. Man did buy a round of drinks . . . must be affected by these new lights.

His cards curled in his left hand, Pops Levansky allowed a reluctant grimace to widen his mouth, since it was his turn either to fold or to ante. Through this he allowed his thoughts to go on, tuned as they were to the banker. The Citizen's Bank was a peanut waiting to be husked, and it had considerable financial assets—items that would certainly be of interest to Rafe Belsing.

"Sorry . . . I was just daydreaming . . ." Warily he snaked a look at his cards, which included three aces. "Nope, no sense trying another bluff." He shoved his cards into the discard pile, knowing he probably held the winning hand as the first of seven cowhands entered the saloon. Right away he knew one of the two older men entering behind the cowhands was the owner of the Box-7.

The noise picked up at this, the bar girls eagerly greeting men they knew were free spenders, men who treated them more like ladies than the run-of-the-mill customers did. And at this, one of the three bartenders came out from behind the bar and went back to add the strumming chords of his guitar to the tinkling sound of the piano. The lights suddenly seemed brighter, the night more promising, at least to Pops Levansky, covertly studying both Carl J. Moore and foreman Stony Abernathy holding court

at a couple of front tables that had been pushed together.

He played a few more hands just to let the rancher
get mellowed out by some drinks, and then Levansky
cashed in the few chips he had left. "I believe the
man I came to see is here, boys."

"Doggonit, Pops, we was just gettin' you broke into
losing."

"Maybe you ain't seen the last of me tonight." He
smiled upon lifting up from his chair. He had sorted
out that Moore was the older man with dignified
features, and he pulled out his checkered bandanna
and used it to blow his nose.

When he got over to the tables where the rancher
and some of his hands and some locals were clus-
tered, the rotund con man waited until he'd caught
the rancher's eye, with Carl Moore smiling back. "I
believe you're the bossman of the Box 7 . . ."

"The missus is bossman, as that's who I take orders
from."

"Women sure can throw their weight around. I've
been idling around town the last couple of days, Mister Moore . . . hoping you'd come in. Name's Rickart,
but I go by the name of Pops."

"I take it from the way you're dressed you're a
sodbuster."

"A game I want to get out of. Got a place up along
Sandy Creek. I did get an offer from Faraday, over
at North Forty. One of his land buyers dropped in,
maybe a month ago now."

"That so?" speculated Moore.

"Trouble is, I've been over to North Forty, where
I buy my supplies. In my opinion, this Faraday has
a bad reputation. My place, Mister Moore, isn't
much. But I'd sure like to sell it to an honest man."

Carl Moore had been squinting ponderingly while

taking in what the sodbuster was saying in words that seemed sincere enough. He fingered his shot glass around and then leaned back in his chair as if coming to a decision. He said tentatively, "I expect you know the going price for a place like yours. Right on Sandy Creek, you say?"

"I surely don't expect you to buy somethin' you ain't seen, Mister Moore. I'll be heading back around sunup."

"Wish I could ride back with you, only there's this cattlemen's meeting I gotta go to. What say I amble out there day after tomorrow? Say, reckon you'd best pardon my manners. Here, avail yourself of this empty chair, as I want to spring for a round. That all right with the rest of you boys?"

THIRTEEN

To Tyler Carradine, it seemed as if a lot of years had been given back to him as the bronc carried him at a chippy canter. His mood was one of easy anticipation. The feeling in him was of a man about to go into battle, the shame of his past no longer weighing him down.

He had trimmed his beard up there on the front porch of that mountain cabin, and Tyler had discovered he wasn't all that bad with a gun, though his draw was a shade slower than he liked. But the important thing was that he could hit his targets with deadly accuracy.

"Facing an armed man will be far different," he said, just to hear the sound of his own voice. He wasn't worried about the coming confrontation with Faraday or the man's gunhands, since Tyler expected to take a bullet or two, and in exchange, take out all the men he could. "For certain nobody will mourn my demise."

The low foothills of the Wind Rivers were giving way to the shimmering floor of the basin, along with a red-streaked butte which told Tyler he was approaching the outer reaches of Mineral Creek. The openness of the basin was something he had come to enjoy, and the high thatch of blue sky sprinkled with various cloud formations. A sound came to him when he rode around the southern reaches of the butte, then he spotted further along where trees marked the creek and the cabin being put up by three men.

Deliberately he reined more to the southwest, as there could be some danger in being spotted by the miners. To them, any lone horseman meant trouble because of all the robberies and killings. He didn't blame them none, not with Jax Faraday over there in North Forty, along with Robinson and that lying mouth of his. Tyler had buried the anger he'd nursed so long toward the men who'd framed him. The vicious, callous murder of Duck Sing had opened the floodgates. It told Tyler the truth about himself: that he had to make a stand, as his running days were over.

When he came to a lesser creek and then a cul-de-sac of brush and willow trees, he rode in slowly to come under shade. Some lark buntings chittered through the leafy branches and took to flight at this intrusion to settle down shortly further along the creek. Out among the bullrushes and reeds redwing blackbirds were hunting for water bugs and small insects, two mallards swam around a creek bend, and the wind was as gentle as it ever got out here. Sighting at the sun through furrowed eyes, he determined it would be dark in a couple of hours, at which time he'd ride on in to North Forty.

"I just hope Chauncey Pardee is alive, as he spoke pretty angrily against Faraday."

After he loosened the cinch on his saddle, the bronc started nipping at dark green grass. Tyler stretched out on the sloping creek bank and tipped the brim of his hat low over his forehead. *And don't forget about Anna Drury. There's a woman who wants a piece of Faraday's hide. A real fine woman . . . someone to . . . no, too late for someone like me . . .* Now he withdrew inside himself, clearing his mind of everything. He felt his eyelids growing heavy and slept.

A frayed smile touched Anna Drury's mouth when one of the card players let some change spill onto her tray. It was around eight o'clock, the beginnings of another long night for her and the other girls at the Carousel Emporium, but what made this night different was that at last Jax Faraday and some of his hardcases had ridden out of town. Still hanging around, though, to ramrod things for Faraday was Harney Robinson, hunkered in since noon at a poker table. Anna figured the way Harney had been putting the whiskey away, he wouldn't last much longer. And once he was out of the way, it would give her the chance at last to get into Faraday's upstairs office.

Working here had thinned her out considerably, so that she had to pin in her dress to make it fit her slimmer form, and her eyes seemed more luminous and had lost that old smile. At times she simply wanted to say to hell with it and pull out. But the sparks had exploded in her mind, telling her that no man, either a dead husband or a damned crook like Jax Faraday, was going to cheat her out of what was rightfully hers.

Most surprising to her had been that strange encounter with saloon owner Chauncey Pardee, just a day after Carney Aker's body had been found in an alley. As was her habit, Anna had saddled up the grulla she'd bought and kept stabled at Bagwell's, spurring into Sunday morning's pale light and out of town. Clad in Levis and boots and a favorite old hat, she soon lost herself in the breaks west of North Forty, having in her saddlebags provisions to last her all the day long. These rides were therapy, balm for her soul, and gave her time to sort out all she'd gleaned during the past week.

"So some U.S. marshals have come in? Why haven't they done something, or is this just another rumor—"

Through her frustration, Anna jabbed spurs into the flanks of her grulla in an attempt to get on to a secret waterhole formed by natural springs seeping out of low hills. This was where she'd spent most of the day in silent meditation, although it surprised her that sometimes her mind would play tricks on her by centering its attention on Tyler Carradine, that raggedy saddle tramp and now the swamper at the Golden Steer.

"What is it about this Carradine?" rang out the frustrated voice of Anna Drury.

"Maybe I can fill you in on him."

Reining up sharply at the sound of that voice, her horse shying around in a nervous circle, she soon picked out the horseman framed between a pair of limber pines, and she blurted out, "Hold it right there, mister."

"Carradine told me all about you, Anna."

"Just who the hell are you?"

"Tyler works for me," Chauncey Pardee said, as he walked his horse down the short elevation and rode up to her. "But he headed out a few days ago . . ."

"On the run again," she lashed out.

"I own the Golden Steer, Anna . . . name's Chauncey."

"By the way, how do you know about this place?"

"Just followed you out here, as my friends told me about these Sunday rides of yours. Figured out here would be a safe place to talk."

"About what?"

"About how to get the goods on Jax Faraday. I

expect workin' for him hasn't been any Sunday picnic. Carradine lined me out as why you're workin' over at the Carousel Emporium."

"If Carradine left," she said, as they rode on in toward the shaded spring, "I doubt he'll come back. I reckon it's too late for him to change . . . not after all these years . . ."

He swung a leg over his saddlehorn and dismounted and ground-hitched his reins. "He might surprise both of us, Anna." He waited until Anna had climbed down from her saddle and then told her about how Duck Sing had been killed. "Just like your husband, he died at the hand of one of Faraday's men. They were good friends, Tyler and Sing. Probably the only friend Tyler Carradine had . . . since he surely took it hard."

Anna absorbed this as she walked on and stared down at the still spring waters, not at all sure that she should believe what the saloon owner was telling her about Carradine. The night they'd spent together came to mind, and inwardly she blushed, and quickly she shed herself of this. Turning quickly, she speared Pardee with hard, contemplating eyes. "You figure there's a chance he'll be back? And if so, why? The man's a derelict when it comes to human emotions. And if he does, to do what?"

"To help us get rid of Faraday. There are others involved in this, a sort of vigilante group."

"You're not gunslingers, Pardee. Those gunhands of Faraday's will cut all of you to pieces and not even work up a sweat. He's gotten too powerful. Even this cattle baron, this Carl Moore, hasn't tried to brace Jax Faraday . . ."

"That's 'cause Moore lives a considerable distance from North Forty. I like it out here, Anna— least, I still think I do. You, now, working over there for this tinhorn . . . it sure must be hard at times."

"Only my hatred for Faraday keeps me going, Mister Pardee. Faraday has this upstairs office. Or maybe he keeps his records in his rooms."

He grimaced through his worry for Anna, then said, "Just you be careful."

But tonight and right here in Faraday's gaming casino Anna Drury knew she'd have to be bold, throw caution to the winds. She knew that Jax Faraday kept a lot of money in his upstairs office, along with most of his records. One of the girls Faraday invited to his rooms at night had told of a little red book. Perhaps it was in here he kept a record of just who paid him protection money, and there might be other things that could incriminate Faraday.

"Hey, Anna, you seem kind of lost tonight."

She threw back at the bartender, "Guess there must be a full moon."

"Yeah, well, girlie, just hustle this tray of drinks over to that poker table. Then help clean up some of the other tables."

Sometime after eleven o'clock, when Anna was parrying the advances of a drunken miner, she let a sigh of relief dance in her eyes when Harney Robinson at last was heading up the staircase. He slept in one of the back rooms, just in case anyone made a try at killing Jax Faraday. Faraday's other hired guns were lodged elsewhere around town. Robinson liked to muscle the bar girls around and had even beaten up a couple of them, but tonight, with that load of whiskey he was packing, Anna knew he'd fall asleep once he got to his room.

Anxious now, but still cautious, since she knew Robinson wouldn't hesitate to kill her, she kept working the tables with the other girls. Some nights she managed to pick up a lot of money in tips and loose change and gold dust. Tonight, however, she'd let the other girls fight over this, still holding onto the words of Chauncey Pardee that she not take any chances.

A fight that broke out between a cowhand and a small party of miners gave her the opportunity to slip out a back door. From here Anna hurried up the back staircase to come out onto the second-floor landing. She drifted back into the shadows when a door opened and one of the girls emerged wrapped in the arms of a miner. When the pair of them found the front staircase, Anna slipped along the hallway, although there was an anxious moment in passing the door of the room occupied by Harney Robinson.

As she'd expected, the door to Jax Faraday's office was locked. But quickly Anna used a key she had stolen and unlocked the door, and even more quickly and to the faster beating of her heart she was in the office and locking the door again. Street light beamed in the three windows facing to the north and onto Faraday's large, oaken desk and other furniture. Boldly she lit a coal oil lamp, her first order of business to search through the desk.

This time it felt a heap different coming into North Forty for Tyler Carradine ghosting his bronc along a dark lane spongy from a recent rainfall. As in all unkempt boomtowns, debris lay everywhere, and Tyler's hoss shied at times when encountering a tin can or an empty bottle. When Ty came in behind the Golden Steer, it was with a deep reluctance, his thoughts centering on Duck Sing.

Dismounting, he unsaddled his horse and then tied it up in the lean-to attached to the back shed, which for some time had been his nighting place. He stood there for a moment, one hand resting on the shoulder of his horse, taking in the muted sounds spilling his way. In him there was no nervousness, something that surprised Tyler, though wariness caused him to unleather his guns one by one and check the loads. They felt good in his hands, about the only friends he could depend on, he reckoned. "Chauncey . . . said he'd line up others to go against Faraday. Hope so." Grimacing, he headed toward the dark back wall of the large saloon.

He went in through the kitchen door to receive a surprised look from a wiry man with greasy black hair and a stubbled face. "Easy" was all Tyler said as he ambled on and sank down at the table where he and Sing had shared many a quiet meal. "Coffee . . . and anything that's hot . . ." Lifting his hat away, he tossed it across the table onto an empty chair.

"Now look, dammit, you can't just come bustin' in here." The man, who was obviously Chauncey Pardee's new cook, came toward the table holding a small paring knife fluttering about as he added, "Just get the hell and gone . . . say, you ain't this Carradine, are you?"

"Could be."

"Yeah, you're him, all right." A grin split the man's mouth open. "I'm Eddie Crane, a miner . . . or was, until them bastards ridin' for Faraday killed my partner and damned near did me in. We've sure been waitin' for you to come back, Mister Carradine." Eagerly he held out his right hand, which Tyler grasped.

"Tyler will do." He smiled at Crane hustling back to pour a big mug full of piping-hot coffee.

"Tear into this first," he said, "while I go get Chauncey."

As the cook hurried out of the kitchen, Tyler unlimbered from his chair and went to the stove to check out just what was available. He was eating beef stew out of a large ladle when the cook came in behind Chauncey Pardee, whose eyes were filled with a lot of unanswered questions. One of them was answered right away, in that Tyler seemed harder of eye and in far better shape than before.

"Old friend, you came back," beamed Pardee. And then he was embracing Tyler as he added, "Doggonit, this calls for somethin' stronger than Crane's bad coffee. Well, Tyler, sit down, and Cookie, feed the man. Now, just how did it go up there?"

It took a while for Tyler to frame his words, since spoken words had been alien to him up in the Wind Rivers, and he watched Chauncey pour whiskey into a glass. "Truth is, I hated to leave. But knew I had to . . . before . . ."

"No, Tyler, you weren't goin' to cut and run again." Pardee sat down across the table and filled his own glass. "I've got a few good men lined up to turn loose when we're ready. Like Crane here. Another thing, I've been keepin' tabs on Anna Drury. S'matter of fact, I followed her out of town last Sunday just to tell her about you."

"About me?"

"Don't look so dewy-eyed innocent, dammit, Tyler. You like her a lot. Anyway, she's got this stubborn streak, just won't quit workin' over at Faraday's place until she gets herself killed, or maybe kills him."

"I could go talk to her." Tyler's eyes lidded in remembrance of the last time he'd encountered Anna in the streets of North Forty.

"My big worry now, Tyler, is that Faraday is out of town. Anna just might . . ."

"Break into his office. Something I plan to do, and tonight's just as good a time as any. Sure some smooth whiskey, Chauncey; obliged." Rising, he put on his hat.

"I could come along—"

"Nope, this is a one-man job. I'll come back here with anything I find. And Eddie, your stew needs more spice and a heap more onions." Fluidly Tyler swung around the cook and hurried out the back door. As he made his way toward Main Street, the words of Chauncey kept beating at him, in that Anna just might do something foolish, now that Faraday was gone.

Just a short distance away, at the Carousel Emporium, and up in his room, Harney Robinson rolled drunkenly on his narrow bed and spilled to the floor. This roused Harney and his anger, and he cursed while rubbing a bruised elbow, awake now in a room laced with darkness.

He was still dressed, except that he had removed his gunbelt. Pushing to his feet, he reeled a little with a careless hand spilling a few items from the dresser top. "Need a drink, dammit," he gritted out. He made his way to the washbasin and splashed dirty water over his face and hair, and then shook his head like a mad grizzly.

"Faraday's got all that choice whiskey in his office . . . yeah, no sense letting it go to waste."

He managed to get into the hallway without further mishap and grabbed the ring of keys nestling in a coat pocket. In the past he could put down a lot more whiskey, his mind bend that of a man who figured he wasn't all that drunk. Harney knew age had done some damage to his body, as had bad whiskey and habits he'd acquired over the years. Soon, he'd decided, he would quit working for Faraday and find a nice, quiet hole to crawl into.

Reaching the door, he found he had to go to one knee to steady the hand holding the key. When he did so, surprise registered in his eyes for the tiny bead of light seeping out through the keyhole. *Faraday ain't here? Just what the hell is this?* Trying the knob, he found the door was locked. Could be, he reasoned, someone had broken in and was ransacking Faraday's office, a deed that would surely be blamed on him.

Stepping back a little, he sprang forward and hit the door so hard it sagged away from its hinges as it and Harney moved as one into the room, startling Anna Drury, riffling through paperwork in the drawer of an old wooden file cabinet. She recovered first, making a break for a door opening onto Jax Faraday's living quarters.

"You damned thievin' woman," roared Harney Robinson, breaking after her. He caught Anna just as she managed to get a window open with a big hand wrapping into her hair. Through her scream of fear he yanked her back, the force of this tumbling her toward a settee and down onto the carpet, and with the hardcase coming in on her.

He kicked at her leg, rasping out, "Damned slut, you'll pay for this!"

She curled protectively away, ignoring the pain, trying to clear her shattered thoughts. He was slowed by drink, and if she could get up, Anna knew she might be able to get back into the office and use that gun she'd come across in Faraday's desk. Crabbing sideways, she leaped up onto the settee and went over it, and then she was breaking for the open door just inches away from Harney's lunging arm.

The big gunhand slammed into the door frame, but he still came after Anna, darting in behind the desk, and realizing her intentions, he dipped a hand to his belt for the sheathed knife he always packed around. Coming on and gripping the knife, he was stopped cold in his tracks by the harsh words of Tyler Carradine.

"Ease away, Harney! Leave her be!"

He took in the man he hated standing just inside the door and an ugly look crossed Harney Robinson's face. He spat out, "What the hell you gonna do, you damned coward?"

"Spill your brains all over the floor, if I have to." Tyler motioned with his six-gun for Anna to come out from behind the desk, and she did, still staring in disbelief at a man she thought had cleared out of the basin.

"She's a damned thief . . . an' should be turned over to the law . . ."

Tyler laughed ruthlessly. "Jax Faraday's the only law around here. Just where is your killin' boss, Harney?"

"Ask Faraday, as I don't know." His mirthless eyes played over Carradine's scarred face. "You're still ugly as sin . . . an' I don't reckon you have the guts to use that gun." At this, Carradine's gun belched flame, the slug nicking Harney's upper arm.

"I'll not ask you again. Where did Fara—"

"Wait," interrupted Anna. "I came across some interesting papers. And there's this little red book where Faraday logs in things. It could be Faraday left the book in his rooms."

Nodding, Tyler said, "Go check it out while I keep an eye on this scumbag." As Anna went into the other room, Tyler stepped over and sagged down on the desk, motioning as he did for Harney to occupy one of the hardbacked chairs. "Now, Harney, drop that knife or I'll bust your knuckles with another bullet."

"I see you're packin' a knife same's me, Carradine," he jeered out. "You any good with it? Or, like always, are you gonna hide your cowardly ways behind that six-shooter?"

"Suppose you just tell me where to find Faraday."

Harney Robinson made a come-on gesture with his left hand and dropped into a knifer's pose and began circling to Carradine's left. His eyes gleamed with sadistic pleasure when Carradine took the bait by holstering his six-gun and reaching around to unsheath a wide-bladed hunting knife. He jabbed out with his knife and laughed as Tyler ducked away. "You're pretty spry for an old ugly son'bitch."

Tightlipped, and with an icy grip on his anger, Tyler parried quite easily the next knife thrust from Harney. They kept on circling, jabbing with their knives, until the blade of Harney's knife sliced into Tyler's coat sleeve. *Close . . . and even as drunk as he is, Harney Robinson is dangerous . . .* Then Tyler was parrying the sudden rush of his opponent, their knife blades locked together, each striving to find an opening.

Harney was the first to break away as he stumbled backward. For the first time, uncertainty rode a crooked trail through his mind. Usually he liked to fight smaller men, and he was finding that Carradine was a little bigger and stronger, and that he'd better end this soon. His breathing was ragged, hampered down as he was by whiskey and a heavy body going to waste. He lashed out, "This Anna . . . a fine piece of tail . . . which I'm goin' to enjoy soon's I cut out your eyes . . ." Then he was sweeping in with a killing determination.

Tyler just stood there and let the man come to

him, his knife at the ready and standing lightly on his feet. He watched the blade of Harney's knife come in low, seeking his belly, the weight of the man behind it, only to have Harney grunt in surprise when his target shifted quickly out of the way and he slammed into the desk and folded over it, with Tyler Carradine pouncing in and wrapping one of his hands at the nape of Harney's neck as he brought the blade of his knife slicing in to nudge against the jugular vein, drawing blood.

"Now, suh, you'll tell me what you know about Faraday!"

A kind of gurgling laughter came from Harney Robinson as he stopped struggling. When he spoke, words and blood spewed out of his mouth. "You damned . . . Reb turncoat . . . Go to . . ." He coughed weakly and was quickly pulled onto his side by Tyler, who now saw the hilt of the knife protruding from Robinson's belly.

"Dammit . . ."

Derision held in Harney's eyes even though he realized he was but seconds from death. "Faraday's out buyin' land . . . him and his men . . . out by Big Sandy Creek. From this homesteader, name of Rickart. A sweet setup"— he coughed weakly, enjoying the moment— "to kill this rancher . . . Moore. Too late for you or anybody else . . . to stop Faraday's play . . . you damned . . . traitor . . ." He went slack, his eyes glazing over to gape sightlessly up at Tyler.

The short but violent encounter with Harney had worn Tyler out some, and he stepped away from the desk, and removing his hat, used the same hand to wipe the sweat from his face. Then he turned slightly when Anna Drury came into the room. "He's . . . dead . . ."

"Fell on his own knife." His glance dropped to the small red book Anna was holding. "That what you were looking for?"

"I guess so, Tyler." Concern paraded across her face. "Are you okay?"

"Just winded some. For a big bag of wind, he was a tough one. We can't stay here, Anna. But there's a place . . ."

"Chauncey's—"

"That's right, you two are workin' the same side of the fenceline. Folks are beginning to come up the front staircase, so we'd best powder out of here."

One of Tyler's boots slipped a little when he splashed through a mud puddle on a dark lane heading toward the back of the Golden Steer Saloon, to have Anna bring over a steadying arm. "That's all we need," she laughed, surprised that she had, since the past few weeks had been a living hell.

More of a surprise, of course, was how Carradine had stood up to that hardcase. For once a man let go, as long as he had, it was a downhill slide into boothill. As for the pair of them, especially Tyler, once they'd entered the kitchen, it held further surprises in the presence of several men, among them, Chauncey Pardee.

"Thank your lucky stars," he blurted out. "We were sure worried about you folks. Move your arse off that chair, McGrath, and let the lady sit down."

Tyler recognized some of the men gathered around him, and a handful more came in from a back hallway. Mostly, they were miners and locals, and if he guessed right, they'd formed a vigilante group. Maybe they could take over the town, now that Jax Faraday and his gunhands were gone. They looked determined enough, and all of them were armed. Tyler said loudly, "I expect Chauncey filled you in about me . . . as best he could. Tonight, I killed one of the men responsible for, well, givin' me these scars to make me so damned attractive to women." He allowed a smile to show, then swept it away. "If the truth be known, Harney Robinson fell on his own knife. But before he died, he told me and Anna here about some sodbuster named Rickart. Got this place along Big Sandy Creek, I gather."

"Yup, supped at Rickart's place, three weeks ago to the day. Just him and his runty son. What you gettin' at, son?"

Anna Drury spoke up. "This is Faraday's book, a sort of log he keeps, I suppose. Came across Rickart's name . . . and that of a Pops Levansky. Right after their names are these red crosses that have been penciled in."

"Mind if I see that?"

She handed the book to Chauncey Pardee, who started leafing through from the front pages, and when he did, Pardee would nod as if unraveling some dark secrets. Through this, his chin muscles would go taut, and his eyes had gotten cold. "You did good, gettin' hold of this book, Anna. A lot of names in here, my friends. Of men who were killed by mysterious means. Seems Jax Faraday has a macabre sense of humor— "

"Just what are you drivin' at, Chauncey?"

He eyed Burl Meader, a local businessman, sent his eyes probing around, and said, "These red crosses are marked after the name of every man that was killed. Damning evidence, I'd say, against Faraday."

"Only thing is, Faraday's vamoosed."

"Not for long."

"Hold on, now," came Tyler Carradine's calm, soft

Southern voice. Someone had handed him a coffee cup, but he hadn't drunk from it, as like everyone else, he'd been watching Pardee thumb through that red book. "The rest of what Harney Robinson blurted out before he died was that a trap has been laid for the owner of the Box 7. Could be this is where Faraday has gone, to this homesteader's place."

"Carl Moore's no fool."

"Don't make no difference," said Tyler. "Him and Faraday are dueling to see just who can buy the most land."

"Get your drift," said Pardee. "If I figure right, Carl Moore will be suckered over to Rickart's homestead."

"A forty-mile ride at the least."

"And we can't wait until sunup to head out."

At Tyler's statement, everyone began jawing at once, eager to go, but with the realization some of them didn't own horses. Through this, Tyler let his eyes hold upon Anna's face. Her eyes sought his with a calm directness, and he knew something was happening between them. This struck at his awareness, and also that it was time to get on the move. Maybe, for rancher Carl Moore, it was short and getting shorter . . .

His voice shouted out, as it had long ago, when he'd commanded the Reb cavalry, "You've got half an hour to find a hoss and congregate out front of this here saloon."

FOURTEEN

Anymore, Rafe Belsing didn't have disturbing thoughts about having to kill his saddle mate back at North Forty. And he sort of liked idling out here at this homestead, either sucking down corn liquor or playing penny ante poker, or trying his hand at fishing along the creek, which in places had some deep pockets.

For meat, they had made a night foray across Box 7 land and culled out a couple of steers, the carcasses of which now were hung high out back of the log cabin and just this side of the pole corral holding their horses. Life was better than average, the only rancor in Rafe directed at their prisoners tied up in the foul-smelling barn. The strategy, as bossed to him by Pops, was that when Moore showed up, Rickart and his son would be paraded out, just in case Moore had met them before.

The two men Belsing had brought along were taking turns as lookout up on a pine-stippled hill northeast of the creek. And generally, Pops Levansky stuck to the cabin, snoring away or playing solitaire with a greasy deck of cards. Though Rafe's pole started bobbing, he didn't want to come out from under the shade of his Stetson, tipped low over his face. They were running low on prime whiskey and his patience was as thin as it ever got. *Stupid to hang in here. Be*

*no problem ridin' over to this rancher's home buildings and
ambushing the bastard. An' Pops is not the friendliest sort.*
Now, with a resigned grimace, he started bringing in
the fish splashing just below the grimy green surface
to find he had snagged his hook into a fairly large
catfish.

"Well, at least I won't have to eat grainy beef for
supper. Don't reckon I'll share this one with these
other slimeballs, either."

About twenty miles to the southwest, a band of
horsemen were loping out of Garnett on the stagecoach road. It was at Garnett that Jax Faraday had set
up a land office run by his operatives. Though he had
purchased one small ranch and some homesteads,
Faraday couldn't stop thinking about the situation up
at Big Sandy Creek. Carl Moore was a foxy old man,
and not one to just ride into an ambush, not before
sending some of his men to scout out the situation.
These and other thoughts about Moore were the reasons Faraday was heading up there.

More than this was the appearance in Garnett of
a railroad agent. A clandestine deal had been struck
at considerable cost to Jax Faraday. The chunk of it
was that Box 7 wouldn't be allowed to ship their beef
on railroad cattle cars. Everything, Faraday knew,
could go sour if Carl Moore took word of this to the
territorial capital at Cheyenne. Now more than ever,
Moore had to be killed.

They had set out just past noon. Now, a few hours
later, it seemed to Faraday, in the testy mood he was
in, that the creek seemed as far away as ever. Common sense took hold now in the form of gunhand
Rudy Maxwell reining in closer to say, "Be risky, ar-
rivin' there on winded hosses, Mister Faraday. Yonder's a waterhole."

"You're right," he smiled thinly, casting a look at

the late-afternoon sun touching upon a thunderhead. "There are some low hills lining along Big Sandy; we'll watch the cabin from there."

"Meanin' you don't want Pops and the others to know we're watching them, I s'pect."

His eyes flared watchfully to the ruddy face of Maxwell, who was a man in his early thirties, and out of Oklahoma. As yet, Faraday hadn't made up his mind about just who would live or die. Could he afford to leave witnesses? For he was on the brink of becoming respectable, once Carl Moore was dead and he sold his gaming casino at North Forty. He would enjoy the quieter life of a cattleman.

"Pops Levansky— how d'ya read him?"

"Never trust a con man, I say." The hardcase reined up just near to Faraday by the creek forking into another, and with willows standing tall as a horse. Both of them swung down, Maxwell turning slightly, for he knew Faraday was about to tell him something.

"It might have already happened over at Big Sandy. And everyone has beelined back to North Forty. So from here on, we keep from being skylined, as Box 7 waddies will be on the prowl. Once we check things out at that homesteader's place, I want you, Maxwell, to cut out ahead of us for North Forty."

"You mean, to take out the con man?"

"Just keep your eye on Pops and the others. We can't go killin' everyone, not this late in the game. Rafe Belsing is kind of closemouthed . . . but still he knows . . ."

Others on their way to Big Sandy Creek were less tolerant about the coming of nightfall. They were led by Tyler Carradine, who'd relegated the immediate responsibility of getting them there to an old-time plainsman named Zach Lankford, and something of a legend up in the Big Horn Basin. Tyler felt comforted by Lankford's presence, realizing in a firefight, the other nine men with them would probably punctuate holes into shadows instead of scoring any hits.

According to Lankford, they were about halfway to Rickart's place. Lankford was riding next to Tyler, casting off a tangy bear-grease aroma from faded-out buckskins. "What made you," Tyler asked, "join us?"

"Bored, son, to tears. Findin' that civilization has gouged her greedy fingers deep up my arsehole an' is ticklin' my Adam's apple. Another thing is, I knew Duck Sing . . . when he was up at Virginia City, durin' gold rush times. Small world." Lankford squinted ahead at something only he had spotted. "Spooked up a mule deer." He spat tobacco juice from his loping horse, a gaunt-looking paint he rode Indian-style. "The words of a dying man . . . maybe this Harney Robinson was just tellin' one more lie . . ."

"Another twenty miles or so and we'll know."

Box 7 rancher Carl Moore still wasn't sold on this newfangled way of holding in cattle called barbed wire. Something neighboring ranchers were getting into, as attested to by a long fenceline he was surveying where his acreage hooked into that of the Tiedown spread. With him was Stony Abernathy, whose main topic of conversation during the day was a corn that was giving his left foot trouble. They sat slumped on their broncs, in no hurry to get on to a line camp, where they'd stay overnight. It was a mellow day; Carl Moore was in a reflectful mood.

The fence had been put up during late spring, much to Moore's naked disgust. But he wouldn't brace his neighbor about it. Instead, he would let his 'pokes tend to his cattle on a ranch of some five hundred thousand acres. "Just might put up some barbed wire around the home buildings, Stony."

Abernathy merely grunted, showing he was skeptical of this statement by Carl. "What barbed wire means is a lot of 'pokes'll be out of work. Including me, maybe."

"Let you go? I'd miss your sarcasm and pug-ugly face."

Slowly they tugged their horses in the direction they intended to go and headed for the western bank of the dry wash, one of several snaking through this part of the ranch. Backdropping northeasterly were the Wind Rivers. Each time they encountered a small bunch of grazing cattle or a bull out by its lonesome, Carl Moore would look over what he owned carefully, checking for any signs of disease that sometimes came with summer. But so far, all he'd come across were fit cattle, erasing some of his worries.

In the morning they would go the rest of the way to Sandy Creek and he'd try to make a deal with sodbuster Rickart. At the town of the same name, when he'd ridden in for supplies, was the first time he had laid eyes on Rickart, a man who appeared to be just another displaced dirt farmer. Carl knew if he waited long enough, the sodbuster would be starved out and leave, and he could simply take over that small hunk of creekfront acreage. But that wouldn't do, in his opinion, since it would be nice to use the sodbuster's cabin for a line shack. *So I'll just offer the man a fair price. Before Faraday gets his hand in . . .*

Squinting through the weathered folds of his face at the lancing rays of late-afternoon sunlight, he picked out a boulder marking a draw they would take up to the line shack set in among small pine trees on a low hillock. Soon they were higher in the draw opening up more, and with three horses idling in a small pole corral hooked to the log cabin whose stubby chimney was fluttering out welcoming smoke. The collie belonging to Mitch Crabtree came wagging out to encircle their horses, and as it began barking, Crabtree emerged from the cabin and ambled over to wait for them by the gate of the corral.

"Howdy, Carl, Stony. Nice to have someone to gab with for a change."

They all laughed at this, as the other 'poke working out of the line shack— a somber man some said would make a fine undertaker— rarely uttered a word, so it was pretty much like going it alone up here. Most of the other hands simply refused to be parded up with Rafferty, and so Crabtree had volunteered. "Got some taters boiling, and the coffee's done. You boys go right on in." He set about unsaddling their horses as the new arrivals sought the cabin door.

In a few minutes Crabtree came into the cabin, and over coffee, Carl Moore began asking questions about the sodbuster he was going to see in the morning. "You think, Mitch, we could use his place for a line camp?"

"Save a lot of riding thataway, Carl."

"That it will," threw in Stony.

"So I'll offer this Rickart a fair price."

"I planned on heading up toward Rickart's in the next day or two . . . to keep our livestock from drifting too far south along Big Sandy," said Crabtree.

"You might as well ride with us." From here the talk switched to ranch activities and the upcoming fall roundup and how many cattle Moore intended to ship out to market. Later on he would wish he'd asked Crabtree more about this sodbuster, since the 'poke would often ride by Rickart's place when checking on Box 7 strays. But at the moment, he was just pleased to be here and have shelter for the night.

Fifteen

The piercing whistle coming from the lookout post told everyone at the homestead to expect company. The gunhand holding on the hill came out into the open a little and gestured down to Rafe Belsing that it was three horsemen, then he slipped back and hunkered down by his Winchester.

Pops Levansky had come out of the cabin hooking a suspender strap and yawning easterly at the morning sun. He ran a hand through his unruly white hair and then put on his sloppy hat. "Time, I reckon, to get Rickart and his son out of the shed. Though it might not be that rancher . . ."

"Got to play it safe," Belsing agreed, as they went together across the barren yard, where Belsing unpegged the heavy wooden door and threw it open. He glanced at Pops, knowing that concealed somewhere in the floppy overalls the man wore were at least three weapons. Then he entered the shed and stood looking down at the homesteader blinking away the bright light spilling through the open door.

Pops said, "All you have to do, Rickart, is go and sit on the porch after we untie your ropes . . . along with that mangy son of yours." He said all this through a friendly smile, but they could see that his eyes held a warning glint that if they tried anything, they'd be the first to feel burning lead.

Rafe Belsing took out a jackknife, cut the ropes away, and stood back to let them rub their aching limbs before both of them managed to stand up. The sodbuster said plaintively, "I don't know what this is all about . . . and I don't care . . . I . . ."

"Shut the hell up," Belsing snapped. He shot Pops a cold look. "I'll park myself just inside the doorway. If it *is* that rancher, the high sign to open fire is you duffing your hat, Pops."

"Just make sure you miss me."

Grinning, Belsing said, "You're a tempting target. My men'll be using their rifles, an' at this close range, they'll rip some big holes in these cowpie men. Okay, head 'em over, Pops." He shoved the homesteader's gangly son toward the open door. "Remember, not a sound out of the pair of you—"

Beyond the lower slopes of the hills standing west of the creek, a tired group of men led by Tyler Carradine lined their horses toward a jagged cut that plainsman Lankford assured them would open onto the place they sought. Three of the men had dropped back with lame horses, and Tyler realized the rest of them were getting awful leery about facing gunslingers. Now Tyler threw up his hand and everyone milled to a halt.

He said, "This draw opens onto Big Sandy."

"Yup," affirmed Lankford. "An' that sodbuster's place is north about a quarter of a mile."

"I'll go on ahead and get the lay of things," said Tyler. "Give the men about ten minutes, then bring them in, Zach." Quickly he rode deeper into the shallow draw and was soon out of sight in a mass of thick underbrush and small trees.

Before long, he could see the walls of the draw lowering and a treeline fanning north to south. Somehow he wasn't riding alone, for prickling at his stomach was a sensation of uneasiness. Tyler had experienced the same thing when going into battle too many times to ignore it, so he sent his eyes probing upward and along the creek. Once he had cleared the draw, he reined to the north, guided by smoke rising over some trees and a low elevation. He kept his eyes probing the hills to the west, looking as they did down upon the cabin just coming into the range of his vision. He was getting edgier, knowing something was wrong, and this caused him to pull in closer to the trees.

Under the shading porch of the cabin, the attention of Pops Levansky was directed the opposite way and on three horsemen riding side by side on the old trail following the twisting creek banks. Before him on the porch steps sat his prisoners. "Now, if any questions are asked, you boys just pass me off as your kindly grandpa come to pay a visit." He leaned forward in the rocking chair and ruffled the boy's hair and through the same smile waved at the incoming riders. "Sort of gettin' used to this old rockin' chair; I'll sure miss it. Okay, Mister Rickart, ease out a little and welcome your neighbor . . . easy-like . . ."

Mitch Crabtree, who rode on the creek side of the narrow lane, said through a pondering frown, "Rickart's got company." They were in past a penned enclosure holding a sow and her young as he spoke, his concern about this causing Stony Abernathy to throw him a sharp glance.

"Kind of funny, an old man like Rickart gettin' into bein' a homesteader . . ."

"I don't get your drift, Stony."

"Well, that's Rickart, ain't it, still up on the porch?"

"Somethin's wrong . . ."

Then the gun aimed by Rafe Belsing sounded from inside the shed, and at this, the cattlemen split away from one another while clawing for their sidearms.

That first bullet had fanned a hole in the brim of Carl Moore's hat, something he wasn't aware of as he and his men found shelter by the pigpen, the horse ridden by Crabtree staggering when an errant bullet plowed into its belly.

Gritting his teeth at the sodbuster and his son sprawling belly-down out in the barren yard, Pops Levansky ducked inside the cabin, cursing out at Rafe Belsing for missing the rancher. Now the rifles of the other two hardcases boomed out, and it got to be tough going for the cowmen.

Nobody realized that a lone horseman had pulled in, in the form of Tyler Carradine swinging out of the saddle by the east wall of the cabin. He'd witnessed the start of it and now knew at least four ambushers were involved. Ty also knew he couldn't wait for the others to arrive as he hurried around to the back door. Lifting the latch, he eased the door open and saw one of them firing through a front window. Tyler called out to a silvery-haired man, "Drop your weapon!"

Stiffening in surprise, Pops Levansky turned slowly, clutching the six-gun he was using in his left hand, a smile fanning across his face as he tried to fix Tyler in his gaze like a snake does just before it pounces on a field mouse. Levansky's other hand was lifting a hideout gun from an overall pocket. "Seems you got me dead to rights." He let the gun drop out of his left hand, seeing the stranger relax some. Quickly Pops took advantage of this in a spin move toward Tyler, his gun just beginning to center on Tyler's midriff, only it didn't work out as the con man had planned, since Tyler's gun barked twice, with both leaden slugs putting holes in the con man's patched coveralls. He let out a gurgle of surprise before falling heavily.

Suddenly Tyler became aware that more guns had opened up, and he blurted out, "Must be Lankford and the others." He broke out the front door only to confront Belsing running toward the cabin, and both men fired together. Again Tyler's luck held when the hardcase reeled drunkenly while firing an aimless shot. Ty let go with another bullet, which hit solidly into the hardcase's chest. As Belsing went tumbling down, Tyler's eyes lifted in concern to men showing themselves on the upper reaches of the hills, and he knew instantly they had to be more gunhands.

That must be the bunch Jax Faraday took with him when he left North Forty. This sure as hell isn't six-gun work.

Tyler holstered his six-gun as he hurried around to his horse and got his Winchester. He went to the back corner of the cabin and let the slant of his angry gaze drift over the nearby hillsides. Those three cowmen, he knew, were boxed in and would soon be dead unless he took a hand in this. Sighting in quickly, he fired at a hardcase wearing one of them big Mex sombreros to have both the man and his hat go rolling down the rocky hillside. Now it turned into a turkey shoot for Tyler, as he took out three more gunhands before bullets came slamming at him.

He ducked along the cabin wall and came in on the front porch, shouting out to the cowmen, "Help will be here in a minute . . . so hold in there! Is anybody hit?"

"Just Crabtree takin' it in the leg," Carl Moore shouted back. "If you spot that son'bitch Faraday, mister, leave him to me."

A bullet hitting a porch support post drove Tyler inside the cabin, where he held in the open doorway. The hardcases, he now saw, were coming in slower, unsure as they were about what they were encountering. Among his men and hunkered in behind a large, flat rock about the size and shape of an out-house laid on its side, Jax Faraday could barely control his growing rage. "How could Belsing miss? This should all be over by now." His voice rose in frustration. "An extra thousand to the man taking out that rancher. You men, strike to the north along through the copse of trees and get in behind them. Come on, there's only a handful of them . . . let's move on down . . . now, dammit . . ."

Faraday held, his men slinking lower down the hillside and the smaller one to the north, and then, as he rose in anticipation of being in on the kill, his eyes stabbed in disbelief when several horsemen appeared on the narrow flats by the creek and veered, cavalryman fashion, to come riding up the sloping hillside, firing as they rode. It was here that Jax Faraday let panic take over.

Through the blued smoke of gunpowder and the heavy rattling of guns he saw men on both sides going down, and this simply unnerved Faraday to the point he began scrambling back up the hill. He could only think that it was a posse led by those U.S. marshals who'd been snooping around North Forty. If so, he had to get back to North Forty before he was spotted by someone and establish a bona fide alibi. He managed to reach the horses tethered low on the north side of the line of hills. Only when he was a few miles to the west did he rein in his horse and rain curses out at the basin.

"How in hell could it go wrong . . . that damned Harney . . . when I hit town, I aim to settle this with the damned fool . . ." Other thoughts came about his having to pull up stakes now and leave, his anger clouding all reason.

Sixteen

Like some of the gunhands who'd managed to get away from the shootout at Big Sandy Creek, Tyler figured he should flee, too, and not meddle anymore in what was happening at North Forty. The only thing was that he couldn't leave; he wouldn't rest easy until Jax Faraday had paid for his sundry crimes.

Some of the gunhands they'd captured alive stated that Faraday had been there, and a lot more. Though rancher Carl Moore and his men had survived the bloody gunfight, two of the men riding with Tyler had been killed. This weighed upon Tyler as he rode deeper into the blackening web of night. Far ahead of him he could make out the hazy glow of lights that marked where he was going, and a grim determination to get there brought him spurring the bronc into a ground-eating gallop.

As he brought the horse in a short jump down from a low cutbank, it went to its knees but recovered quickly, and then Tyler saw the vague outline under moonlight of the stagecoach road and with a lessening of anxiety he cut that way. Reining back, he brought the bronc into a lope again, the mouth of the canyon in which North Forty lay looming in the near distance. He needed time, Tyler realized, to regather his thoughts.

He was absolutely certain that Jax Faraday would

head directly to the Carousel Emporium to find out about the death of Harney Robinson. *With the rest of his cutthroat breed out by Big Piney, this means Faraday won't have more'n a handful of guns backing him up. I wonder if he'll break . . . or readin' him, try to ambush me.* Before he went there, Tyler had decided to check in with Chauncey Pardee. He wasn't about to simply ram in like a locoed bull over at Faraday's. Pardee and others would have to know that Carl Moore was still alive, and Faraday's gunhands were either under arrest or scattering to safer places.

Ty was tired, not having slept for the past couple of nights, and wearily he took to a side street of a mining town ripe with noise and lights. He knew it was getting late, maybe about the middle of the night, and that Pardee, and even Anna Drury, had gone to bed. Or Anna could have left town just to rid herself of any contact with him, Tyler mused.

Always when Anna retired for the night in her new living quarters out back of the Golden Steer Saloon, it was as if Tyler Carradine was there, standing guard. The few personal belongings Tyler had left behind in the shed Anna had carefully stowed away. To cut the dreary aura of the shed, she'd put up some blue-and-white lace curtains.

As with many others, Anna was filled with apprehension and her own fears for those who'd gone to Big Sandy Creek, though most of this was reserved for Tyler. Oftentimes she had gone into the kitchen of the Golden Steer at night and discussed all that was happening with Chauncey and some of his trusted friends. Here she'd learned more about Tyler, and through this, she realized she had strong feelings for him.

Anna sat reading under lamplight at a small, round table a historical book she'd borrowed from Pardee. She found going to bed a useless ritual, filled as she was with worry. Other things came to mind— like the harsh loneliness of going it alone out at their homestead— and she was tempted to go over to the saloon for a cup of coffee and the accompanying camaraderie, even at this late hour. *No . . . hang in with this book for now. Tyler Carradine— just can't let go of the man. You'd think—* She felt a blush go tingling across her face.

To her total shock, the door of the shed exploded inward and a shadowy form swept toward her. Anna's scream died in her throat when a large, dirty hand clamped over the lower part of her face. The table was shoved out of the way by a man wrapping his other arm around her struggling form. The stench of her assailant pierced Anna's nostrils. She was taken outside, where another man stood watch.

At this moment one of the cooks came out struggling under the weight of a large dishpan full of soapy water. He stopped short by the back porch steps when he saw what was happening and started toward the shed only to have a bullet slam into his dishpan, which he dropped. He then fled back into the kitchen. "Come on," one of the hardcases snarled, "let's track outta here before that cook sounds the alarm." Now he followed after the man holding onto Anna Drury until they were a couple of side streets away and heading generally for the alley running behind Main Street.

"Dammit," cursed the man holding Anna, "she tore a hunk out of my finger."

"No," said his companion, "don't cut her throat . . . Faraday wants her alive. Come on, it ain't that much further to his place . . ."

As the hardcases hurried up an alleyway, the anger of those milling around behind the Golden Steer Saloon was becoming grim, as voiced by Chauncey Pardee. "Faraday's got to be behind this."

"But he's supposed to be out of town."

Their attention focused on the doorway of the shed through which Pardee had just emerged. The small group of about fifteen men didn't realize a man on horseback had just pulled in around the saloon wall. He held in his saddle, picking up snatches of conversation, the gist of which seemed to be about Anna Drury. Somewhat anxiously, he called out to Pardee, "Just what is this about, Chauncey?"

"By golly, it's Carradine! You're back, son, but where's the rest of them?"

"I expect making tracks here from Big Sandy Creek." Tyler reined his horse in closer until he was gazing down at Pardee, the horse wheeling a little from others pressing in too close. "There was a gunfight, Chauncey. Some men went down. But we busted up Faraday's gang of killers. Only thing is, he got away. An' from what this is all about, he's back in North Forty."

"Where you goin'?"

Tyler flung over his shoulder, "Tend to some unfinished business." He spurred into a canter once he was clear of the backyard and on a gravelly lane.

As he at last came out onto Main Street, pain rode in Tyler Carradine's eyes, a pain that spoke of his concern for Anna. Jax Faraday now knew that Anna had been mixed up in the death of Harney Robinson. There was Faraday's secret log book, too, which was in Chauncey Pardee's possession and would be turned over to a U.S. marshal. But, pondered Tyler through cold-slitted eyes, taking in the Carousel Emporium upstreet a couple of blocks, both he and

Faraday knew the game was over. *He probably came back to clean out his safe. He should have left it there . . . but no, Faraday isn't the kind to let go so easily. Killing Anna is one last vengeful act of a man with no soul. He's got to be stopped. Now, Major Carradine, no frontal assault on that gaming house of Faraday's . . . as he still has some guns on his payroll.*

One of the hardcases, lurking in a second-floor room facing onto the street, laid hard eyes back upon the narrow expanse of the street thick with wagons and men afoot. The lower windowpane was pulled up and smoke from a handrolled wafted out into the night. His rifle was propped against the wall, and he was on his second bottle of red-eye and bored with all this. What had got to him was that Faraday had seemed to be running scared and acting kind of spooked ever since pulling in. The feeling in the hardcase was that he should look out for his own skin and pull the hell out of town.

"Be on the lookout for a big man with a scarred face. Should be ridin' in most anytime, says Faraday." He brought the bottle to his thick lips and sucked down more whiskey. "This woman we was sent to get . . . turns out she's this Anna, this barmaid Carney Aker was hot after until he got burned into hell. I don't like this . . . not a tinker's damn."

Suddenly, the hardcase's eyes squinted thoughtfully down upon a horseman coming in from the east. He could make out traces of a beard and saw that the man sat tall in the saddle. The hardcase swiped a nervous hand across his mouth. Just like that, the horseman cut away down a side street, the hardcase torn by what to do. Finally, he decided to just hole up here, and, through a sudden sense of foreboding, let what happened happen. *It still don't make no sense Faraday comin' back alone.*

* * *

Anna stared defiantly through her silent fear at a man she would willingly kill. Her face was a solid wall of pain, most of it centered around her left cheekbone, which had puffed up to cut off vision in that eye. The ring Jax Faraday wore on his right hand had done most of the damage to Anna's face. She was tied up to a chair in the main barroom, now emptied out of customers.

Even the bartenders and the whores and bar girls were gone, driven out by order of Faraday. The first beating rained on Anna had come up in Faraday's office. Blows had pelted her face and upper body to leave angry welts, and though she'd tried to fight back, Faraday's insane anger and incoherent words of pure hatred had beaten her into a dazed unconsciousness. She had slept only to awaken into pain and the arcing lights of the coal oil lamps spread about the barroom.

And him shouting at her, "Carradine'll be back . . . damn his black soul."

Slowly, weakly through her pain, Anna fought the dizziness away, aware at this precise moment that her captor had a deeper fear than hers. Her right eye finally focused on Faraday's face, mottled by whiskey and anger. It sank in that ever since she'd been brought here, the shank of Jax Faraday's words had been directed against Tyler Carradine.

He was sitting on a stool placed at the back end of the bar, drinking whiskey, with a six-gun on the bar top. He went on, "I should have let Harney kill him . . . a damned mistake I won't make again." Though he was staring at Anna, his eyes were unfocused and filled with uncertainty. His men were keeping watch from rooms placed around the encircling balcony. Faraday's gold and other valuables were packed; he could simply ride out of here right now. But he knew he couldn't, and impatiently he strode up to a front window and gazed outside.

Then something drew Jax Faraday away from the window toward the main staircase, and then he knew, an inner sense telling him that Tyler Carradine was in the building. A vicious smile tugging at his lips, he moved over and placed the barrel of his six-gun against Anna's cheekbone and snarled, "Won't be long now before him and you are dead." His eyes played up around the balcony; now Faraday stepped around the nearby roulette wheel and went behind the bar, where he picked up a sawed-off shotgun.

Tyler was in the casino, having gained access from the rooftop of the adjoining building. The window of the bedroom he was in had been locked, and he'd simply broken the lower pane and eased inside. It was one of the back bedrooms on the second floor, the narrow bed unmade, and someone had strewn a man's clothes about, the way some bachelors were wont to do. Maybe it had been one of Faraday's hired guns.

Easing the door open, Tyler checked out the long hallway, which proved to be empty. He held his gun shoulder high while taking a gingerly step into the corridor. That third door up on the left led into Faraday's office, he knew, as he thought about how his old nemesis Harney Robinson had died in there. *Glory be, it's awful quiet up here . . . so Faraday must have chased out all his customers. Would he hold Anna in his office? He could have fled, too, taken her with him to hold as a hostage*. Troubling Tyler at the moment was his knowing absolutely nothing about Jax Faraday's makeup, only what others had told him. But he was certain that Harney had told Faraday all about the cowardly Tyler Carradine.

"Maybe," Tyler whispered to himself, "Faraday picked up on that it was me leading those men who spoiled his little surprise party over at Big Sandy. Maybe that's it . . . and he wants his pound of flesh."

The office door, he found, stood slightly ajar, and quickly he had ducked in to level his six-gun around, and from here Tyler searched through the adjoining rooms. From here he closed in on the office door and the upper hallway, his senses more alert to a warning that kept hammering at his mind. He stood gazing ahead at the hallway pushing up to the staircase and the balcony railing to either side, and beyond that to the other side, where another hallway was cloaked in darkness. *She's down there, Anna is, and for me there're no other options . . . So why sweat it, Major Carradine, as you died a long time ago . . .*

Crouching into the hallway, Tyler moved on soft feet toward the staircase and toward a halo of light sweeping the staircase from the lower floor containing the casino and barroom, and Jax Faraday, he realized. The shot that slammed out of the darkness came from behind Tyler, nipping at his shirt collar in murderous intent, and he pivoted while flattening down, firing back at flame lancing from a Colt .45.

Pow . . . Pow . . .

Even as Tyler's gun was sounding, another gun had opened up from the direction of the balcony, probably from one of those doors across the way, and he knew he'd been suckered into a killing trap. But he managed to stumble on and crouch down by the railing. And when he did, Tyler caught a glimpse of Anna Drury, roped to a chair below.

Behind the bar, Jax Faraday pulled back one of the hammers on his shotgun, not having seen Carradine yet, but knowing his men had flushed a man he hated out into the open, and Faraday wanted in on the kill. "Carradine!" he shouted. "Show yourself, or she dies!"

Barely had the words rushed out of Faraday's mouth than it seemed to him an unseasonal tornado had struck in the form of windows shattering inward and the sound of boots as men came surging in through both the rear doors and the main batwing doors. In his confusion, Faraday started swinging the barrel of his shotgun around toward the front doorway, but too late, as the gun held by Chauncey Pardee and two others blazed out leaden slugs. In seconds there were at least fifty men swarming into the casino, a fact that had little meaning to Jax Faraday groping out from behind the bar, the mortal wounded man trying to bring up his shotgun for one final go at Anna Drury. For his efforts he received another bullet that shattered his spinal cord and he was dead before he hit the floorboards.

One of the ambushers had just taken a bullet square in the chest from Tyler's six-gun, the sight of his body spilling over the railing causing a sudden pall of silence as the three other hardcases involved in this laid down their weapons. Tyler let the men spilling up the staircase take charge of the prisoners, his concern only for Anna now.

He came down the staircase to find Chauncey Pardee untying the ropes, saying, "She might be hurt bad, Tyler . . . her face . . ."

Leathering his gun, Tyler nodded grimly as he removed the bandanna that was tied around Anna's mouth. He knew facial bones were broken, even though Anna forced a smile to her full lips; a moment later she went limp, with Tyler balancing her in his arms. He barely heard Pardee calling out for someone to fetch Doc Prichard. Torn now by the cruel fact that he loved this woman, a newfound emotion only increased the anger he felt for Faraday. But the important thing was to get Anna to the doctor, and he carried her outside, following Pardee through a mob of onlookers that had gathered in the street.

Upon receiving word of a new gold strike down in Cripple Creek, Colorado, most of the miners had pulled out of North Forty. Many of the businesses had gone belly up, as the town turned somewhat reluctantly back to its old role of being a supply point for basin ranchers. Jax Faraday's gaming casino had been sold at public auction by a U.S. marshal, the monies of which were distributed among the relatives of men killed by Faraday's band of cutthroats. Then, just a week ago, the Carousel Emporium had burned down, along with some other buildings.

Although the stagecoach still came, as did a few still looking for gold, the seeds of decay were taking hold, something Tyler Carradine took in stride. Actually he welcomed the more peaceful side to North Forty, and like other locals, was making plans to leave— but not until he said his goodbyes to Chauncey and other friends, and of course, Anna.

Much to his surprise, his part in the capture of Faraday's gunhands had resulted in his being given part of the reward money, a little over two thousand dollars, a windfall he carried with him on this balmy Tuesday morning. As he closed in on the Golden Steer, his pace faltered, a sadness and a lot of uncertainties welling up inside him.

During the time Anna was recovering, he'd been up at her bedside. Though she had seemed to accept the fact that her face would be disfigured, as Tyler's was, but to a lesser degree, he sensed that her spirit had at last been broken. And he grieved over this.

In the saloon, he was greeted quietly by Chauncey's new day bartender, a woman named Gladys, who brought back from the kitchen a pot of hot coffee and a plate of food for Tyler, sitting at one of the tables. He was the only customer, and though he sipped from his cup, his thoughts were more on Anna than on his chowing up.

"Let's face it, Tyler, you like her too much to just pull out."

"Nope," he said. "It's just that . . ."

"Quit playing games with your mind, Carradine. Underneath all those scars you carry on your face is quite a handsome man, somethin' you won't admit."

"Now look, Gladys . . ." He choked off the rest of it, stifling his sudden resentment when she smiled. "I . . . I guess in a way we're soulmates now . . . me and Anna . . . I . . ."

"Why don't you tell her that?"

And just like that, Tyler found himself on the staircase and then entering the bedroom occupied by Anna Drury, who he discovered was sitting up in bed and returning his wondering gaze. Awkwardly he removed his hat and rolled it around in both hands. He tried hiding the pain in his eyes when he took in her face and the small scars crisscrossing her cheekbones and the one scar up near the right eye. Then, unexpectedly, he saw her old smile blaze out at him.

And he blurted out, "Anna, got to tell you, I . . . I love you with all my heart. Me . . . well, me and you are the same now, if you . . ."

"In a way we are," she said softly. "You know, the doctor said I could vacate this bed tomorrow. And yes, Mister Carradine, I love you, too . . . only . . ."

"There aren't goin' to be any onlies, Anna. That

is, will you marry me? As I sure don't want to go it
alone anymore . . ."

Her smile was telling Tyler all he wanted to know,
and he came in to sit down and gather Anna into
his arms, letting all the old pain and anger go, knowing that at last he'd come home.

SMOKE JENSEN
IS
THE MOUNTAIN MAN!

THE MOUNTAIN MAN SERIES
BY WILLIAM W. JOHNSTONE